This collection was created with no restrictions on the content ... no restrictions on the authors (any race, creed, color, gender, or orientation was welcome), and no excuses from the editor. It is called *Leatherwomen* because the women who know of and use that name are not yet well represented on the shelves of our favorite bookstores. It's part of the act of throwing some doors open; ... Gradually, more readers will get to see women on the shelves; powerful, sexual, sensual women. Who knows? Any of us might meet a person whose life was transformed by a collection just like this one ...

—*from the Introduction, by Laura Antoniou*

LEATHERWOMEN

**EDITED BY
LAURA ANTONIOU**

A ROSEBUD BOOK

Leatherwomen
Copyright © 1993 by Laura Antoniou
All Rights Reserved

No part of this book may be reproduced, stored in a retrieval system, or transmitted in any form, by any means, including mechanical, electronic, photocopying, recording or otherwise, without prior written permission of the publishers.

First Rosebud Edition 1993

First printing April 1993

ISBN 1-56333-095-4

Cover Photograph © 1992 by Trevor Watson

Published by Masquerade Books, Inc.
801 Second Avenue
New York, N.Y. 10017

To Pam & Liz
For Their Wedding
Because They Heard it First

LEATHERWOMEN

Foreward: *Mad Votaries of Diana* A. Joanou	9
Introduction Laura Antoniou	11
We Never Speak of These Things Maria K. Adar	21
Me and the Boys Trish Thomas	29
Dear Mistress Michelle Dubois	43
Rasp a.k.	59
The Workshop Dorsie Hathaway	63
Don't Get Me Wrong JayCee Sylvana	69
Leather and Steel Barbara Louise	89
Coprolalia C.W. Redwing	101

The Basement Deborah J. Ruppert	107
DDYKNWS Kris Miller and Cubby	113
sammy S. Brosa	127
The Roar of the Sea Denya Cascio	131
Bubbles T. Casey Lively	151
Knife Carol A. Queen	157
The Triangle Lady Sara	167

FOREWARD:

MAD VOTARIES OF DIANA

She was known in the Middle Ages as the ruler of the wild forest. She was devitalized by phallo-centric Christendom and equated with the Devil. She has been called the Queen of Heaven, the Mother of Creatures and the Destroyer. The goddess Diana was associated with the sorceresses that were burned and was said to have led the wild aerial night flights as the Queen of the Witches, and she is vitally alive today in the dark nightclubs of San Francisco and New York. She is dynamically alive in the bedroom and on the streets. She is the guardian of the women who shamelessly devote themselves to the Dionysian shadows and excesses of sexuality, the women who claim themselves proudly unchaste and stand fearlessly undiminished within the force of these wildly sexual emanations.

The women of *Leatherwomen* are simultaneously destructive and nurturing, both tender and cruel, while the authors intrinsically recognize the fact that duality is a dead-end. Their words herald a philosophy of pansexuality and pluralism, a philosophy that ensures political and libidinal freedom for all.

In between the covers of *Leatherwomen* one will find a rare cultivation of seemingly simple objects and words. Within the tactile world of black leather, utterance of safe words become avatars and magic phrases. These are manifestations written with wishes and slaps, and it is the molten core of this unapologetic collection of erotic tales.

The leather chaps, the whip, ropes, clamps and the other mechanisms of SM play become symbols in an allegory that is not simply about pleasure but includes the potency of women's desire for power. The stories become the analects of a contemporary goddess, Queen of the Urban Frontier. Where there are legends of cycle sluts, lurid tales of women in prisons, histories of mistresses in dungeons and diaries of masters and slaves, there is the shade of Diana.

The words of *Leatherwomen* display a fierce dedication to what might be called the more complicated pleasures, and in the practice of this devotion the stories become actively subversive and vital to sexual culture. The act of recording these fantasies and confessions serves to maintain the dynamism of sexuality through constant recreation of the infrastructure, and define different contours of the woman's sexual world. The symbols and the incantations of the safe words and the ritual smell of leather carry the atavistic power that is the clarion sound of a different future.

—A. Joanou
San Francisco, 1993

INTRODUCTION

So what's this leather stuff about?

It seems strange writing an introduction to this book and including a brief guide to the world of the leatherfolk. While collecting stories, I had assumed that the majority of the readership would already know. But this collection will find its way into the hands of a lot of readers who are as unfamiliar with my casual usage of the term "leather" as they might be with 1990s Queer politics. So if you're an old leathermensch[1] yourself, just drop ahead into section two of the introduction. I give you permission to skip the basics.

Leather is largely a euphemism. In different communities it can mean anything from leather fetishism to cross-dressing, from the guys who just like rough sex to the fashion mavens who flock to gatherings like Dressing for Pleasure to check out the latest erotic wear, to SM, which is also known as

Sadomasochism, Sadism & Masochism, et al. Leather as a style and an image owes a great debt to the gay male community, where chaps, motorcycle caps, Sam Browne belts, and engineer boots became totems of sexual potency. Now the leather name and a great deal of the "look" is applied to people of all genders and sexual orientations.

For the purpose of this collection, leather covers not only an image but a drive. Leather by itself is only the skins of dead animals. But, when used here, it is an encompassing world of powers and fetishes; it becomes a way to unite a fascinatingly diverse group of women. It becomes the catch phrase for their most resonant fantasies and secrets. The leather on these women isn't just a jacket or a pair of boots, although that may be the way they dress.

It is the world of their fetishes, the way they enact power exchange, their verbal and mental games, the physical intensity and emotional hunger in their sex-play. It is their courage to break taboos, religious, cultural, social, and personal. It is a journey where, as Oscar Wilde might have put it, you may end up feasting with panthers.

Now for some serious stuff mixed with the reasons why the collection is put together the way it is:

While I was collecting the stories and poems, many women commented on the title of the collection. Many women thought that *Leatherdykes* would be a much cooler title, much more contemporary. I would agree, if that word fit the content of the collection I was gathering. But this is a book about women first, leather/SM second, and dykes only as far as dyke readers can enjoy the content. (And I hope that many do!)

Introduction

Five years ago, Pat Califia caused a few murmurs of dissent with her statement, "Many people do not fantasize about the kind of sex they actually have."[2] She defended (indeed, demanded) the right for lesbian writers to be able to write about fantasies involving men. I remember thinking, "Imagine the nerve of someone telling me what I have the right to do! Imagine having the *chutzpah* to tell me what I have the right to fantasize about! What is this woman talking about?"

I was so naïve! Five, six years ago, I had only had contact with people who thought that my sexuality was just fine the way it was. (Anyone who seemed to think otherwise, I just didn't associate with; it's amazing how denial can work, isn't it?) So I talked about these statements that Califia made with some amusement. Why would anyone condemn another person's very fantasies? I asked. And I remember getting my answers, from lesbians who apparently thought I was "one of them." I remember reactions ranging from mild annoyance to outrage that Califia would dare include stories about men in a lesbian anthology. *Real* lesbians, I was told, do not fantasize about men.

Five years later, I have come across some interesting (and sometimes sobering) facts about lesbians and about groups of women in general, including self-identified bisexual and heterosexual women.

Women who have sex with women fall into many overlapping categories in terms of demographic characteristics, sexual identity, and behaviors. The terms lesbian, bisexual, and heterosexual (or straight) are used to describe sexual identity or orientation; yet sexual identity is not always congruent with sexual behavior. This should not be a great surprise to anyone. But the extent to which we deviate from our identities (whatever they are) may astound you. But first, an important caveat: Many of the studies I have read and quote here come from agencies which collected the data for the purpose of tracking HIV in different populations. And the U.S. government has, through the CDC, tried to minimize the presence of any women who identifies as a lesbian by defining "lesbian" as a woman who has not had sex with a man *since 1977*.

But: in a sample of clients utilizing the programs at AWARE (Association for Women's AIDS Research and Education), women who had had at least one female sexual partner in a three-year period were *more* likely to have engaged in anal intercourse with a male partner than women who had no female partners. More striking is the fact that many more women who identified themselves as either *exclusively homosexual* or as bisexual had engaged in anal intercourse with a male partner than women who identified themselves as heterosexual (32 percent vs. 16 percent).

This is not an anomaly, although the specific style of sexual contact (anal sex) is a little surprising to me. Other studies over the years have reported that as many as half of all self-identified lesbians sleep with men periodically. Kinsey, in 1987, said that 46 percent of self-identified lesbians had had sex with men since 1980. (A much broader range of years, to be sure.) But 32 percent of those women were aware that their male partner was behaviorally bisexual, regardless of the man's own perceived sexual identity. Of those women reporting sex with bisexual men, 45 percent reported vaginal intercourse. And 88 percent of lesbians who reported sex with any men reported vaginal intercourse, and 30 percent anal. *Yet only 8 percent of the lesbians who had anal sex with men always used condoms; less than 5 percent of*

Introduction

the same sample always used condoms for vaginal intercourse.[3]

Outside of the United States, a study of 500 lesbian and bisexual women in Australia revealed that 90 percent identified themselves as lesbian, dyke, or gay, yet 79 percent of the total sample had sex with men. Of that sample, 23 percent had injected drugs; 90 percent had had sex with men.

In a small study of IVDUs in San Francisco, 53 percent of the self-identified lesbians reported sex with men in the past five years, 25 percent for drugs or money.

Am I saying that lesbians really aren't lesbians? Certainly not! Lesbian may mean any number of things to any number of women, from being totally woman-centered, erotically, culturally, and socially, to being politically aware, active, and devoted to lesbian issues. The real issue at hand, and what so many studies have shown, is that lesbians not only *fantasize* about men from time to time, but many of them also have sex with men. And we cannot afford to discount the percentage who do it because they are sex workers or to be able to obtain drugs; I am talking about the behavior here, not the reasons for it.

We should be able to embrace women who behave sexually with any consenting partner of their choice. It does us no good to pretend that some lesbians don't occasionally have sex with men, whatever their justification. It leads only to the self-delusions which make women lie about their activities to their lovers, tricks, and doctors. And I included the amazing statistics about the percentage of lesbians who report using condoms because of this: Identifying themselves lesbians seems to give far too many women a mystical belief that merely doing so somehow lessens their chance of contracting STDs—or much worse, HIV. (Perhaps because of the institutional denial of the possibility that lesbians could be at risk.) Ignoring behavior for the sake of a label can lead to the most terrible delusions; we must stop it. It's that simple.

It also makes bisexual women ashamed, and heterosexual women male-defined by default. Are we, the sexually marginalized, such a large and strong community that we can afford to continually divide the members? Should those who have felt oppressed by societal constraints and expectations develop a new set of guidelines for what (and who) is acceptable, judging them on their *sexual behavior,* of all things?

I have heard many arguments for (fill in the blank)-only space. Woman only, lesbian only, dog-owner-only—you name it. And we should not deny any group the right to assemble and create an agenda according to their needs, services which benefit their members, and activities which will advance them toward their goals.

But we must also learn the hazards of exclusion. I say, *throw the doors open*. The more allies and friends we have, the better off we are. The more self-examination—of ourselves, our activities and concerns, our needs and desires, our fears and dreams—the better off we will be. We should encourage many more visions than absolutes; many more offers of inclusion than restrictions on membership. When we are hundreds of thousands strong instead of simply hundreds, when we can come out of *all* our closets and support each other in public and through our individual political and financial decisions, then we will have plenty of space and time to parcel out to every group that wants its own club-

Introduction

house. And no one will have to be heterosexual, bisexual, or lesbian "just for the weekend."

This collection was created with no restrictions on the content (save that everyone had to be over twenty-one and no one could die), no restrictions on the authors (any race, creed, color, gender, or orientation was welcome), and no excuses from the editor. It is called *Leatherwomen* because the women who know of and use that name are not yet well represented on the shelves of our favorite bookstores. It's part of the act of throwing some doors open; this book will be on the shelves in gay and lesbian bookshops, some women's bookstores, the few leather and fetish stores that stock paperbacks, and the mainstream stores that carry all the popular novels that Americans eat up like Halloween candy. Gradually, more readers will get to see women on the shelves; powerful, sexual, sensual women. Who knows? Any of us might meet a person whose life was transformed by a collection just like this one. Or maybe just one story. When we throw the doors open, we are guaranteeing that there will be no universal acceptance; someone will definitely be offended.

So, just as a warning: if any reader can't handle stories about men, SM, humor, pain, humiliation, bisexuality, lesbianism, power, cross-dressing, heterosexuality, whippings and fuckings, gender ambiguity, bondage and knives, novices, smart-ass masochists, people who just talk dirty and/or wear Girl Scout uniforms, I can suggest only one thing.

Get over it.

Now, what about these women?

I asked the women who contributed to this collection

to provide a biography of themselves that wasn't "standard." My instructions to most of them was to create a 50–150 word bio containing anything they wanted to say. For those who asked for more direction, I suggested that they might include personal information, political statements, or thoughts about the particular work they had submitted. It's interesting to note how they responded.

Most of the women who have been published before submitted standard bios, with a list of other publications which had paid them for their work and one line (or two) about their lives. That line contained where they lived, and what else they did, either for money or as a lifestyle option.

But the so-called amateurs, the women who never had someone ask for their own thoughts about themselves and their work and then offered to have it published for other women to read? Well, some of them really knocked themselves out. And some of what they wrote (stretching the 150-word maximum to the limit), was so interesting and personal that I couldn't bear to edit them down very much. It's important for erotic writers and readers to know much more about each other, and not only in terms of what the market demands. We are exposing ourselves and each other; we need to be able to place it all in context. Though some of the names are false, the fantasies ring true. We are in an alternate universe of erotic potential.

Some of the authors revealed that events in their stories were based in reality; others cheerfully wrote down their most powerful J/O fantasies and shipped them off with sticky pages. (Uh ... thanks.) They run along an uncharted course which lands at several taboos (rape, for example) and puts in at familiar ports of call (love letters and humorous vignettes).

Introduction

Introductions and brief biographies come before each story. Dedications, if any, follow them.

You may now enter the den—or climb out on that limb. *Bon appétit!*

—Laura Antoniou, 1993

Notes

1. Leathermensch is my own word for leatherperson. *Mensch* is a wonderful Yiddish word which translates roughly as "human" (no special gender applied), but there is an additional meaning to it that is less defined. It also means an upright, honorable person. The best leatherfolk are leathermenschen (pl.)

2. Pat Califia, *Macho Sluts* (Boston: Alyson Press 1988), Introduction.

3. From the Lesbian AIDS Project of GMHC, NY. One term used to describe this phenomenon is the "Lesbianism as Condom" theory. It is reportedly "nearly as common among health-care professionals as among the at-risk clients."

MARIA K. ADAR

A vast majority of submissions to this collection and to magazines publishing erotic material deal with new lovers or playmates. Part of the thrill of the story will tend to rest in the discovery of new sensations or acts. But people do have hot scenes and/or sex with their long-time companions. And the value of a long-term relationship shouldn't overshadow the passion the partners have for each other.

The power in "power exchange" is one of the greatest aphrodisiacs in the world. Maria K. Adar, a native of Quebec who describes herself as "just a regular lesbian who happens to own another regular lesbian" has managed to capture the awe of a magnificent SM relationship from the viewpoint of the top.

She says: *It was hard to imagine what to write at first. After all, from the point of view of the sensuality, it's the bottom who gets all the joy while the top does all the work. Just describing a scene from the top point of view seemed strange and almost cold. I kept wanting to get into the head of the bottom and show what was "really" going on. But then, I realized that the action isn't necessarily what makes a relationship hot. And the largest sex organ is the brain.*

WE NEVER SPEAK OF THESE THINGS

Her eyes asked me, "How does it feel?"

How does it feel when you answer the phone and I can hear the joy in your voice? As though we were still courting, getting to know each other's smell and taste, and that for you, every phone call from me is a new chance to get to know me, a surer step toward Saturday night. I hear that you are always happy to listen to me speak, always flattered to know that I want to talk to you, and always disappointed when my voice is captured on your machine and you weren't instantly available to hear me.

I am so pleased when I walk into a room and you are there, wearing the clothes you know I like to see. I can imagine you standing in front of your closet, pulling the outfits out one after the other, holding things up to the mirror, wondering if they will be right. I see you tossing clothes on the floor in frustration, running to the bathroom to make sure your makeup isn't smudged.

And I know that you arrive at the bar hoping I'm there, waiting for me to come in, and that your attention is scattered and impatient until I come near you. I feel a hissing of breath between my own teeth when you stand for me, coming to attention of your own free will; and when I come close, I know that you will shudder at the friendly touch of my hand. I am awed that my recognition means so much to you.

And when I take my hand and grasp the back of your neck, feeling those two points that can bring you up to your toes or down to your knees, and I can feel the shaking, the tension, and then the relaxation of your entire being, I am bemused. I can feel every shift in emotion as cleanly as a temperature gauge. You make no effort to hide them. You make me smile.

I am always aware that your eyes are on me, your ears turned to hear my voice. When you follow me like a loyal dog, I know that you are hungry for the slightest nod, a touch, a word. I am careful when I grant them. I pull you close suddenly, to hear you gasp. I tempt you with my posture, sometimes unconsciously, and I see the need in you to fall at my feet, curl by my leg, draw your body in close by my side. When I finally do point or press your shoulder, I know that between your legs there's a wetness growing, and you are trying to control yourself. I know that when you stand, you want to kneel. When you kneel, you want to grovel. When you grovel, you want nothing more than to be utterly prone, my boot against the back of your neck, squirming against the floor.

I am always aware of that. So I control it, in myself and in you, so that each progression never loses its magic. And I delight in knowing that you know what I'm doing, and that you always struggle with your desires, trying to be strong.

I feel the great power that holding your dignity grants me.

And when we are alone, and you alternately lower and raise your eyes, waiting for me to take the lead, patient yet barely holding back your desire, I feel like a monarch. I know that you will leave me if I choose, unfulfilled in your lust but content to spend mere time with me.

I know that I can simply use you for my pleasure, or even lie back and command you to please me and then send you away, your cunt overflowing, your head spinning from the service you offer. And I know that you will remember every moment of those nights, that you will replay them over and over in your head, making them the crux of your most private cums, and you will love them with all your soul.

Or I may choose to put you through an ordeal, tormenting you with those things you hate, teasing you and causing you discomfort and pain, until your writhings tempt the real sadist in me and I can only push you deeper and deeper into the mire of your own fears. I can poke and thrust at you until you make sounds that shame you, until your body responds and fails you, until you cry out those words you hate and finally surrender, utterly. Not to me, but to the pain, to the shame, to the fear that you will break and I will not find you interesting anymore.

And although I cannot even imagine such a time, I feel the fear from you; and when I am a sadist, I drink it like brandy. Or tears.

Or I may be kind to us both, and bring out those things which we both love, and feel the ease of play. I know that you will breathe in the rich scent of the leathers, eagerly hold your limbs for the binding, turn your body for the lash. I love to see your shoulders bracing against the heavy tresses of my whips, and feel the fire building beneath your skin. I am so proud when I hear the strangled cries of pain that you allow to escape, knowing that you can remain silent if you choose, yet you will display these reactions for me. I know what they cost you. I know that you endure more then you should, to allow yourself the freedom of such grunts and sighs of pain.

I love it when your body is bared for me, and I can possess it, every inch of it. I can spread you out, wide open, your cunt a doorway for me, my fingers, my hand, my tongue, my cocks, my vibrators, the handles of the whips. I love exploring it, with gentle caresses and harsh slaps, with pins and clips and pincers, and with silken ropes and wraps and brushes. I love it when you strain against the ropes and the only thing I hold is a slender nylon rod, or when you squirm and twist under the touch of a feather. I love watching you, your hand slowing, drawing near that open cunt, when I've told you to please yourself, and you close your eyes against the bright lights I have trained upon you. I tell you that I will take your picture like this one day, and you cum.

Oh. The rapture of your shameful obedience, your terrified lust.

I am captivated by the way your body welcomes me. When you bend and I can open your ass and slide in, I am mesmerized by your sighs, the easy way you accept this most intimate violation. When I fill you to the point of pain, I can hear your breath catch and hold, that little whimper of submission, acknowledging my right to hold you so, begging for just a moment to adjust. I know that you will take more, and I know that your allowing me to choose is but one sacrifice in a long line of sacrifices. I press inward, my eyes fixed on your opening hole, my ears on those little whimpers of fear and gratitude.

I am amazed at how much you trust me, that you will put your body and your mind into my care and deny me nothing. When I command you in an act you have never done, you are more then willing; you are eager to do it, and do it well. You are genuinely sad, sometimes angry, when you cannot take what I have planned, or complete a task I have laid upon you, or enjoy an act I request. And I am touched when I hear you try to hide your resignation, as though you think I don't know you. But I do know. I know that you will do as I say despite your pain or your shame or your distaste, until I tell you to stop, and then you will bask in the slightest reward.

I remember that I was once torn between commanding you to difficult tasks for your pleasure in performing them, or laying them aside in my respect for your tastes. Now, years later, I know that I will never stay a command for your sake. Doing so robs you of your chance for a masochistic, obedient martyrdom.

And sometimes, I feel confused. At the emotions you bring out in me, at the ways you've made me rethink. You make me into a tyrant, a monster, who dines on your suffering and drinks your strength. I am never so wonderful in your eyes as when I grind you into the dirt, leaving marks of scorn on your body and soul. You depend upon me for approval, yet wish for my anger. You always want and need more from me; yet as time passes, you make yourself content with less. I want to reward you, make you happy. But to do so, I must punish you and make you feel like nothing.

I don't know how I do this. But somehow, when I am with you, it all comes out of me. I am overwhelmed by my own hungers, all responding to yours.

I want to own you, to possess you, to mark you with my spirit. I want to raise you up as my most precious thing, not my lover, not my girlfriend, not my slave, not my submissive, not my bottom, not my toy, my boy, my girl, my pet, or my thing, but just absolutely *Mine,* for as long as we live.

I am honored by your devotion and loyalty. I am humbled by your patience and strength. I am awed by your faith in me, and your ready obedience. I am made whole by your love.

We tell each other these things every time we meet. We never speak of them.

TRISH THOMAS

When the sex is radical to begin with, it takes just the slightest nudge to send it spinning into a new dimension. Any leatherwoman worth her boots will recognize the kind of moment that is so excellently captured in the line: "I want him the way a perverted, horny bulldagger wants a young, tender drag queen in a tight black slip and combat boots...." It's just one of those things, that's all. Trish Thomas offers a roller coaster of sensations in this remarkable story. It's captured the attention and recognition of several other anthology editors, and we can only hope that she has enough future work to share around. You can find some of her writing in such publications as *Frighten the Horses*, *Taste of Latex*, *Bad Attitude*, and *Logomotive,* and the anthologies *The Best American Erotica, 1993*, (Colliers/McMillan) and *Dagger* (Cleis Press). And as for the author personally, Thomas is a career-minded, patronizing, officious, adversarial prima donna ... or so her bio states. I dunno, I thought she was nice.

ME AND THE BOYS

I don't know what's up with me and boys lately, but alla the sudden I want one. Not just any boy, a faggot. And not just any faggot, a drag queen. And not just any drag queen, Dreamboat. It's crazy how this shit works, but sometimes, outta the blue, my cunt starts doing my thinking for me because my brain can't handle what my cunt is telling me to do. That's how this whole thing with Dreamboat got started.

There we were one ordinary day, hanging out, drinking coffee, and smoking cigarettes like usual, when I got up to go take a piss. Right when I got back to the table he stood up to go himself and bam. I was frozen in time. My pussy started humming and for a split second I wasn't aware of anything except the length of his body, right in front of mine, and the fact that I suddenly wanted to grab him and pull him against me. From my head down to my toes, I was on fire. It didn't show on my face, I made sure of that, and he went on to the bathroom without any idea that I came this close to slam-dunking him right there on the table in the middle of the coffee shop.

I sat down and lit a cigarette. By the time he got back to the table, I was normal again. Naturally I didn't mention my flash of desire for him because he's a faggot and I'm a dyke, and my brain was back in control, and my cunt can't talk.

I tried to put it outta my head, but now I was looking at Dreamboat in a whole new way. Every time I'd see him after that, I wanted to jump his bones. Not only that, but I started having alla these dreams about him. The dreams were pure mush. All we ever did was make out and hold hands. It got so I was embarrassed to wake up in the morning. So embarrassed that I've been forced to develop full-blown daytime fantasies just to save face. Fantasies that range from clandestine, passionate kissing up against the walls of public bathrooms to putting a leather horse-bit in his mouth and pulling back on the reins while I fist him from behind, doggy style, on the kitchen floor of his apartment, where his roommates could walk in and bust us at any moment.

Then that started freaking me out, too. What's a nice butch dyke like me doing fantasizing about a drag queen with a dick? But you know, so few people really turn me on that it seems kinda silly to get hung up on a gender thing. Besides, if I fuck him, I'll still be a dyke because that's what I am. Simple. I don't want him the way a woman wants a man. I don't even want him the way a fag hag wants a fag. I want him the way a perverted, horny bulldagger wants a young, tender drag queen in a tight black slip and combat boots, which is what he had on the day he really took me over the edge. The day my brain said fuck it and gave in to my cunt. But that came later. I'm getting ahead of myself. First there was Pretty Boy.

Now, Pretty Boy is actually a girl. Not in the way that Dreamboat is a girl. Pretty Boy is a girl with a pussy. A girl who looks like a fifteen-year-old boy, so naturally I was attracted to her right off.

By the time I took her home, I was way overdue. I hadn't picked up a girl since I quit drinking. Forgot how. Plus which, the idea of being caught naked in the same room with another human being, without the help of five or six kamikazes, scared the living shit outta me. It was starting to look like I was never gonna fuck again, but I refused to give up. One night, I did it.

Bolstered by sheer horniness, I think about what I want and scan the crowded bar to see who can give it to me. Not the blond—too femme and too innocent. She wouldn't know what to do with me. Not the girl with the overgrown mohawk who's leaning against the wall. Too wasted. She'd probably pass out before we even got going good. I know how that goes. And not the one who just planted herself in front of me. No pizzazz. No edge. No challenge.

Her. Up on stage. Wrapping up the mike cords from the band that just finished playing. She's shorter than me and smaller, but she looks sturdy. I bet she can hold her own. I move closer to get a better look. She's got a boy's hands and a boy's torso. No breasts that I can see. She's wearing a Thrasher T-shirt and faded black jeans that hang loose on her hips. Her hair is short and messy. She looks like she just got outta bed. I wonder if she got fucked right before she came to work.

She looks up and sees me staring at her. We've talked before but this is different and she knows it.

She can tell from the smug expression on my face and the angle of my head that I've already looked her up and down, assessing her. I don't approach her. I give her time to think about my silent offer and decide what she wants to do. It doesn't surprise me when she comes over later and sits down next to me.

A mixture of shit and lube drips down from her asshole onto my thigh. She's on her knees. Her face is smashed into the pillow. Her wrists lay still in the small of her back bound by leather restraints and locked together by a snap-hook that's attached to a long chain that runs over the base of her spine, down between her less, up under her belly, between her tits, and up to her throat, where it stops, padlocked to the leather dog collar that she wears around her neck. Each time she rears her head and bucks up against me, the chain pulls tighter across her cunt.

I'm sitting behind her on the bed. Her ass is marked with my fingerprints from the night before; inches away from my face, right under my nose, I'm working a butt plug into her asshole and pumping a dildo in and out of her cunt. I'm mesmerized by the smell of her and the rhythm of fucking.

I leave the butt plug in place and put my hand up to her mouth. She pulls off the latex glove with her teeth and I throw it on the floor with the others. We've been going at it for three days, stopping only to eat and sleep and piss and shit.

I pick up a leather paddle and start smacking her hard on the ass, alternating sides, while I keep pumping the dildo into her pussy. The sharp stinging that rushes through her torso really gets her going. When she's finally finished coming, I ease the plug out of her asshole. It's caked with shit. I slide the dildo out of her cunt. It's covered with blood. I snap the hook off of her restraints, bring her hands up to the top of her head, and lay them on the pillow. I lie on top of her and grind my pelvis against her hips. The clean cock that's strapped over my pussy slides in and out between her thighs.

"I want you to suck me off."

She turns over onto her back and sits up. I've lost all track of time and become aware of the rising sun only because the light coming through my bedroom window lets me see how red her lips are as she closes them around the cock. I love watching her do this to me just like I love watching her eat. The way she opens her mouth with no hesitation every time I offer her food from my plate. Hungry. And willing.

I reach behind her head and pull hard on her hair, just to see her mouth fall open. I push her face into my crotch. I rock back and forth on my knees, fucking her open mouth. Underneath the harness, my clit gets hard. The inside of my cunt is soaking wet. I'm getting ready to cum, but I don't wanna cum like this. Some butches are too butch to spread their legs; I'm too butch not to.

"I want you to fuck me."

I unbuckle the harness and pull it out of the crack of my ass. She slips it on over her own thighs while I turn around and put my ass in her face. She lubes the cock and holds it in her hand, rubbing its tip up and down my cunt from behind. I think I'm gonna pass out if she doesn't give it to me soon.

"Fuck me, you bitch."

That's what she was waiting for. She shoves it all the way inside me with one easy thrust. I can see us in the mirror that's at the head of my bed. Jesus, we look good. She gets a grip on my thighs and pushes the cock deeper into my cunt. She fucks me for what seems like forever. Jesus god this is good. I cum once like this, but I'm not done yet.

"I want your fist."

She pulls out and I turn over. She reaches behind me and takes two gloves out of the box on the headboard, puts one on each hand, and smears them with lube. She lifts my legs into the air and slips her thumb into my asshole. My eyes close, my back raises up off the bed, and my muscles loosen to take her in.

I open my eyes and watch her face while she gives my cunt one finger, two fingers, three fingers, all four fingers. Just like that. Even though she's done this to me many times already, she's still amazed by the size of my pussy. She winces when she gives me her whole fist. She can't believe I take it so easily. I don't move. I'm savoring the feeling of being completely full with this fag girl's hand.

I plant my feet on the bed and push my hips up to her. Now I want it hard. She uses her whole body to give it to me. I'm staring at her. Looking her right in the face while she takes my entire pussy with her hand drives me outta my fucking mind. I'm gone. I'm outta this world. Everything is outta focus. I've given myself over.

I pull her hand out of my asshole. She knows what I want. She leaves her fist in my pussy but stops stroking it. She slaps me in the face. My nipples get hard. I slap her back. I don't know why slapping the woman who's fucking me turns me on, but it does.

My hands drop down between my legs. She stops slapping me. She pushes her fist to the back of my cunt and starts stroking again. I push my hips against her and use my hands to work my swollen clit until I cum. When I do, she pulls her fist out real slow. She lies next to me on her side. I roll over and lay my belly against hers.

Me and the Boys

"I like what you look like when you're getting ready to cum."

"What do I look like?"

"Like an animal."

Me and Pretty Boy have been doing it for a few weeks now. She matches me fetish for fetish. What a lucky fucking break. Still, I can't seem to shake this vision of riding Dreamboat from behind with the horse bit in his mouth and the reins in my hands. I want it all. I don't have the balls to hit on him. I'm used to getting what I want, but frankly, I'm afraid I'm outta my league with this one. The guy's a faggot for chrissake. What if I come on to him and he laughs in my face? I don't know.

I don't know, but here I am at Sunny Leather and I got a little extra money in my pocket so I pick out a horse bit and take it to the counter along with a couple bottles of lube and a box of latex gloves. I'm waiting for my change and out of the corner of my eye I spot an empty pair of combat boots in the dressing room to my left. I get my change and back up, real casual, to the magazine rack behind me.

I pick up a magazine and pretend to leaf through it. The curtain on the dressing room is halfway open; from this angle I have a perfect view of the girl inside. Her back is toward me. Her legs are long and lean and slightly bowed. She's wearing black stockings with seams and a red garter belt. Her thighs are solid and curve sweetly into a nice, round ass. Her back spreads in a perfect V out to her broad shoulders. I can't see her face yet cuz she's pulling something on over her head.

Oh my god, it's Dreamboat. My pussy thumps.

He pulls a black satin slip over his hips and smoothes out the hem. He turns to one side and then the other, admiring his profile in the mirror. My pussy starts to throb. He rubs his hand over his crotch, and I can see his cock getting hard. He lifts up the front of his slip and starts to stroke it. I watch it get thicker and longer. My cunt has almost convinced me to go into the dressing room and have my way with him when the owner announces that the store is closing. Dreamboat stops what he's doing and strips. He shoves the stockings and lingerie into his pockets and walks out of the store.

Now, Dreamboat dressed like a boy is one thing. Dreamboat dressed in tacky drag is something else. But Dreamboat in a tight black satin slip with a stiff cock is a whole nother story. I follow him home.

He walks up to Market Street and heads for the underground. He's got on headphones and he's oblivious to everything around him, so he doesn't notice me. I wait 'til he's on the escalator before I put my Fast Pass in the slot and go through the gate. I walk down the stairs at the opposite end of the platform. We're the only two down here. He thinks he's alone and starts dancing around. I lean against the wall and watch him. I want him.

Three outbound cars come at once. He gets on the first one, I get on the last. From where I'm sitting I can watch all the doors and I see him get out at Castro Station. I follow him up to the street. I'm right behind him but he still has no idea he's being followed. He heads down Castro and goes into the Walgreen's. I drop back and pretend to look into the store windows while I wait for him. Oh shit, there's Pretty Boy at the ATM. I duck into a doorway and peek out. Pretty Boy walks away from the ATM and crosses the street in the middle of the block. She gets into her truck and starts the engine. Whew. She didn't see me. Good.

Me and the Boys

I look down the street just in time to spot Dreamboat coming out of Walgreen's carrying a small package. He crosses Castro and continues down 18th Street. I'm on his tail again. He makes a left at the next block onto his street. I lay back a little now. I stop to light a cigarette while he walks up the stairs to his flat. He puts his key in the lock, opens the door, and goes inside. I climb the stairs and try the doorknob. It turns. Excellent. I open the door a crack and see him heading down the hall toward the kitchen. He stops at the bathroom and goes inside. I toss my cigarette over the railing and slip in the front door, closing it behind me. I step lightly down the hall to the bathroom. The door's open. He's standing in front of the toilet. He unsnaps his fly, pulls out his dick, and starts to piss. I come up behind him and drop my bag from Sunny Leather on the floor. My pelvis is on his ass. I put one hand over his mouth and the other hand under his dick.

"Don't move."

Not only doesn't he move, he stops pissing midstream. He's scared.

"Don't stop. Piss in my hand."

He does. I slip my hand under the bib of his overalls and wipe his piss on his chest.

"You always leave your front door unlocked?"

"Only when somebody's following me."

Son of a bitch. I turn him around and shove him against the wall.

"When did you first see me?"

His face turns red and he looks down at his feet.

"When I was in the dressing room. When you were pretending to read the magazine. Before I grabbed my dick."

He gets hard again when he tells me this. He looks up at me and smiles sheepishly.

I lean back against the sink and take a quick survey of the bathroom. An empty Fleet's enema box is in the trash. His pockets are bulging with stolen lingerie. The bag that he brought from Walgreen's is laying on the back of the toilet. I pick it up and look inside. Disposable razors.

"Getting ready for a night out?"

He blushes again. I open the pack of razors and take one out.

His dick starts to sway up and down and he takes a deep breath.

"Come on," I say, and I grab my bag and walk into the kitchen. I sit down on the table and prop my feet up on a chair. I lean forward, fold my hands, and rest my elbows on my knees. He's still standing in the doorway of the bathroom. I motion with my finger for him to come to me. He walks over and bends down to kiss me but I push him away. He looks at me, confused. I can see he's nervous and doesn't know what to do, so I tell him.

"I wanna see you in that shit you stole from the store."

He loosens up a little; now he's in familiar territory. He unhooks the straps on his overalls and lets them drop to the floor. He leans back against the refrigerator and pulls his boots off. He picks up the overalls and takes out the slip, the garter belt, and the stockings, and puts them all on. I stand up and offer him a cigarette and he leans forward gracefully for me to light it. A strap falls off his shoulder. Standing in front of me is six feet of white-trash girl-boy with short blond hair and big, dark-blue eyes, holding his cigarette like he's a society lady at a big-money cocktail party. Poised and delicate and dignified, he waits for me to tell him what to do next.

"Sit down."

Me and the Boys

He sits on the edge of the table.

I walk over to one of the cabinets and take out a big bowl. I carry it to the sink and fill it with warm water. I grab a towel and a bottle of soap and carry everything to the table. I put my hand on his chest and push him back, lift up his legs and spread 'em. I pull the slip up past his ass and lather the hair around his asshole. I take out two gloves and put them on. His dick starts swaying again when I pick up the razor. When I'm done shaving him, I wash him off with the warm water and dry him with the towel.

I grab the front of his slip and pull him up to me hard. Both of the straps snap and the slip falls down to his waist. I kiss him on the mouth slow and soft. He sucks on the ring on my bottom lip like it's a pacifier. I pull him down to the floor, still kissing him. I smear lube on one of my hands and pin him down while I slide two fingers into his asshole. He takes them both, no problem. I fuck him slow with two fingers for a while. He starts to moan and grabs his dick. I pour more lube on my hand and add my other two fingers, one at a time. I've got all four fingers in him and I'm fucking him a little faster now. He takes my hand off his chest and pulls my fingers into his mouth like he's sucking a cock. Sweet.

I take my fingers out of his mouth and his asshole.

"Turn over."

While he's getting on all fours I take the horse bit out of the bag and lean over him to put it in his mouth. He bites down and I draw the leather reins behind his neck. I pull his head back so he's facing the ceiling while I move into his asshole again with my hand. He's panting. His head is in the air and his back is swayed. He rocks his ass into my hand. His asshole is open wide. The walls inside are smooth and wet with lube and some leftover shit that the enema didn't get. He's really moaning now, and I work my thumb in alongside my fingers. His asshole opens wider and wider until my hand practically falls in. I'm in up to my wrist. I push in a little farther and his mouth drops open. I let go of the reins and the bit drops on the floor.

"Say my name."

He whispers it.

"Say it again, louder."

He says my name loud over and over again like he's in a trance. His voice keeps getting higher. It's late and it should be dark but there's a full moon tonight and I can see my arm pumping into his asshole. I've never fisted anybody in the ass before and it's an amazing feeling. Every time I slow down I can feel his pulse from inside and I gotta gasp for air. My pussy is throbbing for attention. He grabs his cock and starts jacking himself off. I can't see it but just thinking about his big, thick cock makes me wanna pull out my hand and nip him over before he comes and it's too late.

The kitchen light snaps on and floods the room. Oh fuck. Not now. I know in my fantasy I wanted Dreamboat's roommates to walk in and bust us but not any more. This is too sweet and too raw for an audience and I'm not ready to stop. I turn my head and look behind me. It's not his roommates, it's Pretty Boy. Fuck. Now what do I do? What's she gonna think seeing me kneeling on the kitchen floor behind Dreamboat with my arm halfway up his ass and him whinnying like a stallion?

I look back at Dreamboat who's shooting cum onto the floor. I look back at Pretty Boy again. She unbuttons her fly and her cock drops out. She pulls a rubber out of her pocket and rolls it up the cock. Excellent.

MICHELLE DUBOIS

In gay male SM porn, specifically in daddy/boy stories, there is a format involving a letter home. The boy has either gone or been sent away, or perhaps the daddy has taken a trip, and what happens in daddy's absence is the basis of the story. Here, Michelle Dubois, in her first published story, uses the same format to tell the tale of a girl who has been given a sojourn in a boardinghouse/school run by three dominant women. Dubois, at twenty-three years of age, wishes that there was such a place to go to; she'd go for her vacation every year. But so far, news of such an establishment has not reached her in her native Louisiana.

She says: *I am physically new to SM and powersex, but I can trace my fantasies back to when my older sister and I played pirate games and fought over who got to be tied to the mast and tortured until she gave away the hiding place for the jewels.*

Yeah, didn't we all?

DEAR MISTRESS

Dear Mistress:

Thank you so much for the package you sent me, Mistress! Mistress Janet says that she's never seen such beautiful detailing on a pair of wrist cuffs, and they fit perfectly!

i am so sad to be away from you, but i am so happy that you found me such a wonderful place to stay. The other girls are very friendly, except when they are instructed not to be. And i have already learned quite a bit. i'm sure that by the time you get home, i will be much more valuable to you.

For example, yesterday we all learned how to make gentle hand movements instead of flailing our arms around "like windmills." It was just like dancing, the way we all lined up in the studio, surrounded by mirrors. Some of the other girls are much better trained then i am. i don't want to embarrass you, so i try my hardest to be as perfect as possible. But when i am surrounded by such lovely women, all naked and moving delicately at the command of a perfectly serious Mistress, i feel like a little girl in a wedding party. Everyone else seems to know what they are doing; all the other girls seem to be in perfect control of their behavior. i know i will never achieve their level of expertise, Mistress, and i am so grateful that you spare your precious time to be with me.

You asked that i write down all that has happened to me, and how i felt. Well, Mistress, i feel very sore right now! i am writing this letter while kneeling on the floor; Mistress Laurel does not allow any girl to use the furniture. But i don't think i could sit down anyway. But please don't be very angry, Mistress! i will explain what happened. i know you will see that i am being treated exactly as i deserve, and that you will not need to repeat these lessons!

When i arrived at the airport, Mistress Laurel met me, as planned. She instructed me to be silent, and i was, all the way through the airport, and then to her car. But once we got in, i didn't have to make an effort to obey her, for she immediately gagged me and then blindfolded me. It was so terribly exciting, being taken away like that, not knowing where i was, and being unable to utter the slightest sound! And you know me, Mistress. i could barely keep still. But i did! All the way to the House. i tried to imagine what would happen if we were stopped by a policeman, whether Mistress Laurel would deal calmly with him and leave me draped and bound in black leather at her side. Would he ask her what was going on? Of course he would. And perhaps she would tell him, and then he would want her to prove it.

i thought of her undoing the gag so i could say, "i

am here of my own free will, sir." And i thought that the policeman would be big and strong, and that he would want to touch me. i thought of being held by Mistress Laurel, feeling her fingers drawing my blouse open, or pulling my skirt up, so he could see. And then the rough, hot feel of his hand, pinching one nipple, or even approaching my pussy. i wondered if i would hate it.

All these things kept me busy on the long ride to the House.

As you explained to me, my clothing was taken away and i was collared before they even took the blindfold off. Thank you for your kind instructions, Mistress. Without them, i would have been so afraid. Instead, i was fascinated. i kept trying to imagine what kind of woman fit the voices i heard. But before they removed the blindfold or the gag, someone (i later discovered it was Mistress Janet herself) discovered what had happened during that long car ride as a consequence of my active imagination. For of course, i was very, very wet. my thighs were soaked with my juices, and a little line ran down one leg. Mistress, i almost made squishing noises when i walked.

It was so deliciously humiliating! One at a time, three women touched me there, and they all were displeased!

"She's got a river down here!" one exclaimed.

"What a saucy little wench! What cheek!" another added.

"What talent," Mistress Laurel commented. (i knew her voice by then, Mistress.)

Well, Mistress, they decided that i should be beaten right away, in the very hallway of the House. They sent one of the other girls for one of the wooden paddles you spoke of, with the leather covering on one side. And with no ceremony whatsoever, they turned me arse-up over a padded bench placed in the hall for this very purpose and all three proceeded to punish me! For my own poor natural reactions to my situation! i know i deserve all my punishments, Mistress, but i must admit that i felt very confused and afraid as it was happening.

They used this paddle over my entire rear, catching me from the upper thighs to the top of the curve of my arse. First Mistress Laurel took me in hand, to deliver what i counted as thirty-five moderate strokes. i was well warmed by the time she was finished with me. But then Mistress Catherine gave me another twenty, and i began to make awfully undignified squeaking noises into the gag. The warming had begun to burn when Mistress Janet stepped behind me and delivered the final thirty. Despite my terrible, muffled cries, she was relentless. Mistress, i cried into my blindfold, and at that moment i would have given everything i have ever owned to be at your side again. i felt alone and afraid. i needed your strong arm and your beautiful hand to soothe me. But it wasn't to be.

Mistress Janet then freed me from my position and my blindfold. She exclaimed when she saw my tears and immediately summoned another girl to come to her side.

This girl was taller than me, with a much larger bosom. Her blonde hair fell down around her shoulders in thick, heavy curls, and she wore a collar that proclaimed her to be Stacy's Slut. Oh, Mistress, when i saw her, i wanted to bury my face into her breasts. (You know what a weakness i have for them!) But i instantly remembered that you had a friend named Mistress Stacy—and do you know, Mistress? This girl, whose name is Marly, is one of her slaves! She is

Dear Mistress

here for some schooling, though, not just for boarding.

But i digress. Marly was brought over to me and commanded to kiss my tears away. Apparently, this is a custom here, for the girls to taste each other's tears. It was a gentling, calming experience, my Mistress.

But it did nothing to ease the throbbing between my legs! In fact, my beating had only served to reawaken my lust, and i had added yet more moisture to the pool already gathered there.

i know, Mistress. i am truly incorrigible!

But no one checked my condition after my beating, and instead i was forced to bear the gentle kisses of Marly, her breath sweet and hot, her naked body pressing into mine with a force she surely did not need to create. When the Mistress commanded her away, she looked once into my eyes, a sharp glance that communicated amusement and interest. My knees weakened, but i was able to remain standing as the three Mistresses explained the rules of the House to me. i was finally able to look upon them all, and Mistress, you were never so right as when you told me that these four weeks were going to be the sweetest torture of my life.

Mistress Laurel is every bit a Lady of business, her narrow face a study in clear thinking and dispassionate decision-making. She is the voice behind the directives of the House; her rules are the ones taught to every girl and posted in every room. You know how she appears, Mistress; indeed, you instructed me in recognizing her, but you did not tell me about her steel-gray eyes, or her elegant stride. She commanded my attention and obedience at once.

And Mistress Catherine, your old friend ... you didn't tell me, Mistress, that she was so beautiful! i can barely breathe when i am near her, Mistress.

How powerful she is, with those broad shoulders, and how strong her grip is! It was no longer a wonder that she gave me fewer taps with that paddle then her companions did. No doubt she was very concerned with possibly damaging a girl. But i would pay the penalty of such damage, Mistress, if only to be at her mercy for one session. To be able to collapse between those long legs and caress her powerful hand with my lips, i would gladly consent to a little damage on my worthless body. i thought that when i first saw her and i think it still, Mistress. i am so glad that she is your friend!

And of course, Mistress Janet, the Lady whose House this is. Oh, she is a great Mistress. The other two defer to her with such elegance and devotion that they seem servants themselves, if that is not an impertinent observation. Her voice is so soft and gentle, yet it carries with it an authority that cannot be denied! When i see her, Mistress, i can only feel like falling before her, falling completely prone and begging to lay the lightest kiss upon her instep.

i was instantly overwhelmed, my Mistress. In truth, i cannot remember how i got to my new bed, or even how i met the other girls. i only remember being told to sleep after such a long journey and start fresh the following morning. And i did my best to follow instructions, Mistress, despite the burning between my legs. It took me a long time to stop from tossing and turning, my hands itching to soothe my lustful urges, my heart crying out for you.

But eventually, i did sleep. i dreamed, Mistress, of your voice, soothing me in the darkness.

i do not remember what woke me up the following day, but i remember that i was having one of those dreams you have just before you wake up, when you are almost sure it is a dream, but not sure enough to wake up. i was seeing myself tied to your table, Mistress, at a party, like the one you had at New Year's. And i dreamed that you had invited everyone there to make use of me, Mistress! i dreamed that everyone wanted me, and that their hands were all over my body, and way, way in the back of the room i could see you, smiling.

So it was very, very difficult to pull myself awake. But reality proved more demanding then my lustful desires in the dream. i snapped my eyes open upon hearing some sound or another, and i found that every girl in the room had gotten out of her bed and was standing in a peculiar position. Their naked bodies shining in the early sunlight, they were all bent at the waist, their upper bodies suspended over the surface of the bed, their arms extended out and down to brace themselves on the edge.

On one side of me was the white posterior of a girl whose bottom showed six clear cane marks. As she shifted back and forth in place, i could see that her pussy was shaved clean, just like mine, and that she had two little gold rings on the outer lips, one on each side.

On the other side, i could see Marly, her huge breasts hanging down, her head bowed.

Perhaps i thought i was still dreaming, for i failed to rise immediately and assume this strange position. This was, naturally, to my great detriment. For Mistress Catherine came into the room with an explosion of activity, her long strides carrying her immediately to my bed. i opened my eyes all at once and stiffened, but i did not pull away, Mistress, nor did i cause her any difficulty at all. Not even when she took me by the hair and pulled me out of bed, so i landed hard on my rump, all tangled in the sheets.

So i was punished for oversleeping, Mistress.

How? Well, i was bound into a cunning arrangement of bolts set into a doorframe on the west side of the dining room. And while all the other girls knelt on cushions and ate their breakfast with careful, ladylike bites and soft murmurs, i was forced to watch, a large gag stretching my mouth to the fullest, and a much larger dildo held in my pussy by a wide strap which buckled around my waist. Little decorated nipple clamps hung from my tits, with bells on them, so every shift i made earned me a mysterious mark upon a chalkboard posted by the other door. i was to discover that i made these little silver bells ring thirty-six times during breakfast.

i thought that my bondage and humiliation was to be the end of my punishment, Mistress, but i am sure you know what happened next. At the end of the meal, when the dishes were quietly taken back to the kitchen and the girls had cleaned themselves, Mistress Laurel came into the room with a bowl containing folded slips of paper. Each girl took one slip from the bowl and held it until the Lady nodded. At once, they opened and read them. And then each girl turned to me and smiled.

Written upon each slip of paper, Mistress, was an act. They were, on this morning, Kiss, Pinch, Spank, Lick, Thrash and Penetrate. i know now that some other interesting acts which dwell within that bowl include Slap, Penetrate (Rear), Caress, Nibble, Strap, Suck, Cane, Lash, Tickle, and even Cut. Marly tells me that the Mistresses change the contents depending on a girl's training and limits, but even so it is a terrible thing to be sentenced to a Punishment of the Papers.

For after breakfast, each girl was to bestow upon my poor, helpless body, thirty-six of the actions written on her sheet of paper. When i heard this issued

Dear Mistress

from the stern mouth of Mistress Laurel, i was sure that i had ascended to heaven, Mistress. After all, i thought (in my abysmal ignorance!), how terrible could thirty-six kisses be? Or thirty-six licks? i thought that thirty-six "thrashes" might be worrisome, but i was so sure that i could bear them that i only sighed into the gag when the sentence was announced. i was soon educated.

The first girl who was led to me held the slip which read "Kiss." Gently, oh, so gently, she kissed each of my aching nipples, still crushed in those beautiful clamps. The bells rang, partly from her touch and partly from the shudder of pleasure which ran through my entire body. i knew at once that i could endure not only thirty-six such kisses, but three hundred and thirty-six! i was so wrong!

For she stayed right where she was, Mistress, alternating back and forth between my breasts, and each kiss was longer and harder then the last. Her wicked tongue darted out to wrap those tender nubs and draw them into her mouth. She compressed the nipples so much that when she turned from one to the other, the one that was merely clamped felt comfortable. Yet the intense joy of each kiss was as excruciating as the steady pain. Back and forth, from one breast to the other, until there was nothing in my ears but the pounding of my heart and those awful silver bells!

Eighteen kisses on each bud left me shaking, gazing down at the shiny red areas that were not covered by the pads of the clamps. The air seemed suddenly chilling, and my nipples were so terribly erect that they felt ready to burst.

The next girl showed me her paper and then proceeded to pinch me, with hard, twisting little movements of her narrow fingers, all along the insides of my thighs. Each grasp of flesh made me squeal behind the gag, and despite the agony of her grip, some of my juices began to flow around the enormous dildo still in my pussy. She felt them and laughed, her light voice a taunt i could hardly stand. But i kept my legs apart, Mistress, as i was ordered to do! Even though some of the pinches she gave me turned black and blue, i did not move away from her, not one inch! Well, i shook in my bonds for a while, and the bells did ring a little, but it wasn't on purpose. i hope my intentions count!

It was Marly who showed me the slip which commanded a spanking. So i didn't get to see her as she walloped away on my rear end. But Mistress, she has a hand as heavy as any lady disciplinarian. And her aim was perfect. In thirty-six smacks to my arse, she landed eighteen directly in the center of each cheek, until i had two red-hot circles just the size of her palms, burning away quite merrily. The bells sang, Mistress, as Marly swatted my behind. For each shot drove me forward, to the very limit of my bonds, and i was compelled to stand up straight after each one, to prepare for the next.

By then, Mistress, i was more than ready to deliver up my orgasm. In fact, it was so close to that point of no return that i was having trouble breathing; they removed my gag for a minute to allow me to regain some control. Then it was put back in.

"You are not permitted to cum," Mistress Laurel said sternly. "You will behave!"

i wanted to cry then, for even as the words left her mouth, another girl stepped up and unfolded her piece of paper, which read "Lick." And, with a deliberate slowness, she sank to her knees, and brought her fingers up to my sex. Carefully but firmly, she pulled apart my lips. The dildo in me, held in place by an arrangement of straps, seemed exposed and vulnerable to the slightest touch. Her action made me squeak, and there was more laughter about the state of my body. With consummate skill, she bared my clit and brought her sweet mouth over it. Even the warmth of her breath was agonizing! i wanted nothing but to clench my thighs tightly together and pull away. But i stayed as still as i could, Mistress, i swear it!

And without letting her lips touch me, the girl began a series of thirty-six slow tongue-lashings right on my clit. And they weren't just slow, Mistress, they were rough. Each time she pressed into me with passionate strength, and the movement of her tongue almost seemed like sandpaper. And because she was very careful, there was no rhythm, no steadiness, and no telling when the next one would come! And she avoided touching the base of the dildo as much as possible, but i was stretched open wide, and the width of the toy put more pressure on all my pleasure spots.

Mistress, i was happy to be gagged, because if my mouth were free, i would have been begging for release. i would have taken responsibility for everything gone wrong that entire day, from my waking up tardy to the chilly weather. i would have offered anything, promised anything. But oblivious to my erotic sufferings, the girl made sure that each of the thirty-six licks was harshly delivered, directly on target.

By the time she was through, i felt like a wreck. i wasn't sure if i could survive the morning, let alone my weeks at this house. But i had not cum—i held onto that threatening orgasm with every bit of strength i could muster.

The next punishment was a Thrashing. In this

house, that means a beating with a short, fat whip with a lot of tresses. The girl who showed me her paper was dark-skinned and hauntingly beautiful, Mistress, although her beauty does not compare with yours. And when she hefted the whip, i could see that there was power in her arms.

Every part of my rear not already made red by Marly's spanking, was now reddened and made sore by this girl's most energetic "thrashing." And she continued beyond my cheeks to catch that tender area just below the curve of the ass, at the top of my thighs. Each thump of the whip made my thighs compress and my hips jerk. i was aware of nothing else but the fire in my sex, filled but not satisfied by the fat dildo i was wrapped around. i felt like i was fucking the thing, Mistress, but that its own movements were designed to severely limit my own pleasures.

i think that was when i started to cry.

The final sentence was penetration, Mistress. i think you know what happened. For the final girl stepped up, showed me her paper, and then donned a cunning little harness. Then, she carefully detached the arrangement of straps holding my hot and now-dripping wet dildo in my body and slowly drew it out. i screamed as i was emptied, but i knew it wasn't going to be long until i was filled again. Carefully, and in my sight, she affixed the dildo to herself, and then stepped up close to me.

As she slid into me, filling me again, i started making incredible noises into my gag. They were part scream and part sob, with a little of hysterical laughter thrown in! i meant no disrespect, Mistress, but the combination of pain and pleasure, the teasing torments and the hard disciplines, drove me a little insane. As she started to move, counting the strokes, i knew that i only had to hold out for thirty-six of them, and then the punishment would be over. But the evil part of me wanted nothing but the release of an orgasm. As the girl pushed carefully into me, holding my waist to support herself, i cried, tears spilling down my cheeks and blurring the details of her face. i began to count as well, doing it backwards, forcing myself to concentrate on anything but the sensation of being filled and fucked.

You know i had to fail. By the time my count reached ten, i was panting for breath behind the gag, and my whole body was washed with sweat. my heart was pounding so loud i couldn't hear the girl counting out her own numbers practically in my face. Instead, i tensed and then relaxed and then tensed again, working with her pace, and feeling each stroke as the number dwindled. Nine, eight ... it began right then, Mistress. Seven, six ... i shook, pulling at the bonds, my hips thrusting back to meet hers! Five, four! i cried out your Name, Mistress, over and over again, my pussy clenching and pulsating, my nipples so hard that i couldn't feel the clamps anymore, and i twisted and humped my way through the final three thrusts.

When the girl pulled away, i was dripping in sweat and sexual juices.

When the Mistresses took me down, they scolded me quite severely and sentenced me to three more punishments, for achieving orgasm without permission. And Mistress, at lunch and at dinner, and again just before being dismissed for one half an hour to write to our Mistresses and Ladies, i was beaten. And that is why i must write to you on my knees and why i must sleep on my belly tonight. my poor arse is aflame; i have been chastised to my limit, i am sure. But i am repentant, Mistress, i truly am. i shall be up on time in the morning, and i shall be the first to be in position, i promise you!

i love you and miss you, Mistress. Enjoy your vacation, and please desire me when you return. i remain most faithfully yours....

A.K.

Fetishes are a major part of the mysticism of SM and leather play. They defy reason, which makes poetry an appropriate vehicle for their exploration. a.k. is a bottom-true from Indiana whose major loves are costume fetishes and "forbidden fantasies" (whatever they are!). This is her first appearance writing about her eroticism.

She says: *I'm used to writing pretty poetry about sunsets and women's eyes, when what I really wanted to scribe were odes to boot polish and strong dykes with long legs! I'm not quite ready to cum out yet, but when I do, there will be a lot of dykes with happy feet!*

RASP

The little ridges
under my tongue are neat,
machine placed stitches holding you imprisoned
behind sleek ebon armor.
Reality is entropy
when all there is is plain, shiny black, and
all i am is running over all you are.

The firm surface is
wood, layered and lacquered and
tasting of salt and grit
and this is where you land, and this is
what makes you so tall,
so big in my eyes.

LEATHERWOMEN

Heavy and wet. Filthy as night.

Steel curves make
the pressing hard, and the wash is
smooth over a sea of skin,
lips feeling heat, praying for warmth.
Eyes closed to blackness, scent rising.

i am drunk with you.

DORSIE HATHAWAY

In a social milieu where women are as likely to meet attending a lecture on codependency and SM as they are at the local bar, there's a willingness to share private joys in public. Women who have felt objectified or ignored in arenas of social sexuality have found different levels of comfort in sharing their passion in settings where they are valued but not priced; where they get to be the center of attention yet not be the obsessive goal of dozens of selfish voyeurs.

Dorsie Hathaway describes herself as: *a Lesbian writer, lover, fighter, dreamer, mother bear, femme switch, and goddess-wannabe. I live in the beautiful Pacific Northwest, and travel the electronic highways in search of lovers and kindred spirits.*

THE WORKSHOP

Portland, Oregon

"So when are you going to see your New York lover?" Toni teases me at lunch. I grin broadly, and she laughs out loud at the look on my face. New York called late last night; the sound of her voice turning me immediately submissive.

We negotiated this months ago. You ran an ad for a pricey workshop, with twenty attendees. Despite the steep fee, there is a waiting list. This will cover my airfare and then some. Friday morning I'm flying.

New York City

We go to the club at night. The bouncer sees you coming, holds the door, familiar and deferential. I am already collared. You lead me into a room full of women and introduce me as the evening's entertainment. In an aside, you bid me disrobe. I obey, eyes downcast, submissive to you.

You are speaking to the group. Very informative, teaching tone, matter-of-fact ... while we are about to commence this incredibly intimate act. I am alternately hot and self-conscious. We share the rich pleasure of knowing I will do anything you bid. You lead me to the table in the center of this room. There is a spotlight here, and I cannot hide in shadow.

At your signal I climb onto the table. Using padded cuffs, you secure my ankles to the stirrups there. I am comfortable and yet completely exposed. I do not look at any of the women.

You're talking now to the group about the bottom's comfort and the importance of good lighting. You snap your fingers, and a woman brings a gooseneck lamp. At your direction, she positions it. You turn on the light and focus it directly on my cunt. Some people move to get a better vantage. The heat makes me warmer and I'm sure everyone can see me dripping.

It's all I can do to hold still when you smooth on the glove. I want this and feel no shame. I want them to watch, to see how hot this really is. I want to create an image that will burn in their minds, gnaw at them, and keep them awake at night. Most of all, I want you to take this gift of trust and see what we can create together, taking my body to the limit.

Your eyes barely connect with mine. I recognize the need for detachment in this setting and accept it. This is a workshop, and you're the teacher. I am, in this room, subject, object, teaching tool. You continue with a clinical discussion of fisting safety, covering gloves, lube, and vaginal health. Your left hand rests on my inner thigh, stroking it absentmindedly, as you would your cat.

The Workshop

The warmth of your hand is comforting. For a second, I imagine us alone, the joy in your eyes as you enter me, enjoy me, connect with me. I am suddenly flushed, dripping, in this room full of women, witnesses, students.

They are standing closer to the table now, eyes intent on your hand and my cunt. You pour a generous amount of lube on your hand and my cunt. You begin touching me, first with one finger, then a second, teasing my cunt open slowly as I writhe. I want all of you, I don't want to wait, I am so hot for you. You take no visible notice of this impetuosity. Later, I think, you will exact a price.

You're still talking coolly about the angle of approach, knuckles, the importance of timing. I think I'm ready to fuck your hand, eat it up, take it all in, but you still have just two fingers in me. This will be a demonstration to remember. You're going to draw this out, tease me, make me wait until I'm fully open and ready to take your fist.

You slide a third finger inside me, and start really fucking me, slowly. I am so wet and ready, wanting it twice as fast and deep. A hint of a smile plays across your lips now as you continue lecturing. You pleasure and torture me in front of these witnesses, and I start panting, "Yes, yes." The witnesses are wide-eyed and very quiet as you push deeper into me. Now you talk about feeling the cervix, about dimensions, and move your hand left and right, turning your arm slightly. I am focused entirely on your face, willing you to look at me and connect for a moment, full circle between vision and sensation.

Four fingers fill me now, and you move your arm back and forth, willing, insistent, demanding. You pour more lube onto your hand and my cunt, and suddenly I'm very open, ballooning inside, transformed. As you fold your thumb into my cunt, the group lets out a collective "aah" and I am at your mercy.

All eyes are focused on this miracle; your hand disappears deep inside my cunt. I am almost breathless, feeling all of you, my insides expanding to make you welcome.

You're discussing the way it feels, where physical limitations come in, about taking one's time. What you're not telling about is how good it feels to possess me, how hot it is to take me down and touch my core.

You fuck me deep, rocking me, hand buried beyond your wrist, and I can't hold still anymore, I'm fucking you back. The women in the room are breathing hard. I take still more of you, my consciousness suspended between your face and the hand that fills me.

You are smiling now, as are the women around the table smile, eyes wide, and finally you speak directly to me, commanding, low, "Come for me." I let go all reserve and focus on your fist in my cunt, still rocking me, and come, yelling. You keep your hand there and I come over and over, until there is no more.

Applause. Curtain.

JAYCEE SYLVANA

JayCee Sylvana is not the real name of the author of this story, and she wants readers to know that. Instead of giving me personal details about where she lived, how, or with whom, she explained why she wanted to write this story this way.

She writes: *I've written erotica under two other names. One of them is my own. The other was so I could break into a different genre without everyone assuming that all my work was going to be the same. But there was always one thing I wanted to read that women's porn wasn't delivering. I get off on the raunchiest, most awful rape scenes. I mean the kind you find in books like* Daddy's Slave *and* Gang Banged Waitress. *I like the stories in the men's magazines like* Drummer, *that feature some pathetic straight guy being forcibly fucked by a gang of studs until he's nothing but a pair of fuck-holes dribbling cum and spit. And there just wasn't a lot like that in the women's collections. So I've written it, or something like it. It made me wet while I wrote it. Now we'll see how many women are like me.*

And, how many women will be *so* offended that JayCee will be glad she wrote it under a pseudonym.

DON'T GET ME WRONG

Let me make one thing clear before we start, OK? I am straight. That's right, a cocksucking woman, a woman who likes the feeling of a big, strong man pumping away in her, a bitch who's had cum spurt up her snatch, in her mouth, and up her ass. Yeah, I took it any way I could, and I liked it. Not like some frigid bitches who just lay there and stare at the cracks and water spots until the guy's finished. I mean, I got into it, the minute I felt a dick sliding into me. As far as I'm concerned, there's nothing like a big hunk of meat being shoved in and out one of my holes until I just cream all over the fucking place. I like guys. I like their cocks.

In fact, that's part of the situation, you know? Because I once had a boyfriend, and he had a problem with Aich, and his problem led to my apartment being a stash for all kinds of bad things. I wasn't stupid; I knew he was fencing the stuff he found so he could shove it up his sleeve. But he was in control, you know? He didn't have a problem with it. A lotta people don't know that most sess addicts, or like they say now, IVDUs. have real lives, they go to work and they have friends and kids and all that happy shit. They really just wanna be left alone, get some stuff in them, and keep right on going. But not everyone lives by the old live-and-let-live code, you know? And I guess Phil's problem was that he didn't always have the cash, so he'd pick up anything that wasn't nailed down and trade it for some green. So he was busted with some slightly used stereo equipment, and I was busted because the rest of his stuff was topped off with a gun he thought he could trade for about a week of heaven.

I guess everything would have worked out if I'd testified against him. The DA offered me a nice deal, but you know, one week apart and all I could think of was how Phil was doing without the smack, and whether they're giving him decent meth, and if he missed me. But I swear to you, sister, if they got me that first week and made the offer, I would have walked and shoved my walking papers right up his sorry ass. But they let me sit too long, and I got to missing him.

See, that's how I figure I'm straight. But we got that settled, so let's move on.

Six months' vacation guaranteed at a upstate correctional facility, with an option to renew if I was a bad girl. That's how my fuckin' court-appointed put it when he said *"adios."* Fucker. I went in figuring I needed a real badass attitude, because I never been up before. I caught a few overnighters downtown back when I was in the Trade, but you know the deal. My daddy had three bail bondsmen on call, and he would even pay for a cab home. But there's no future on the street. And when daddy got 'shroomed in the Bronx because a couple of kids decided to argue with their pieces, I just kinda drifted along, waiting for a new opportunity. And that's when I met Phil, see?

So anyway. I go to the island in that junky bus with the bumpy back seat full of PR girls talking Spanish and the evil-looking black mama who took her man apart with a kitchen knife and five girls who got nabbed because their honeys are just bad news. They didn't talk to me, not much. I was too white, what with my red hair and everything. I heard the word *"puta"* when I walked down the middle and took my seat, and I shot back, "With your old man, slit!" And then one of the guards started banging his nightstick against the window bars to get us to shut up.

I was scared shitless, I can tell you that. All the way there, all I could think of was those shitty TV movies where some blonde white chick goes to jail and there's a million mean, mother-killing lesbians who fuck you up the ass with a broomstick or a Coke bottle, or they catch you in the showers and beat the shit out of you for fun. And then there's the boy guards, who want blowjobs after dark, or in the laundry, and trustees who will make you go down on them for three days so you can get off of disciplinary reports. Man, I was ready to puke by the time we saw the outer gates. I was wondering how the fuck I could manage to stay in solitary all the time and not extend my six months into the usual year.

But you know, it's not like that, not really. At least, not at first. The first week, especially for a new girl, is all exams and getting to know your way around. They look at your eyes, they take your blood, they look up your snatch and up your ass, they even poked around in my mouth, checking for hollow teeth or some shit like that. I actually roomed alone for three days before they got me assigned to a regular cell, and that's when I met Candi.

With a name like that, you know she's a hooker, so we hit it off right away. She was black as night, but man, we had a lot in common. For the next two days, we swapped John stories, talkin' about our best and worst tricks. I mean, she brought back some real funny memories for me. Like the guy who didn't want to fuck but liked to watch a girl jerk off. Now that's not so rare; I used to get a lot of those. They liked the red bush, you know? But this guy, he'd wanna play this really weird music while I was clit-whacking. He'd bring this little Jap radio with him and put in a tape, and what played was that music they always play at the Fourth of July. You know, the one with the cannons and shit. And he'd yell a lot, usually "Yes! Yes!" over and over again, and tell me to hold onto the cum until some big bang.

Like I was really cumming for him, right?

What the hell, he paid good money. Candi liked that story. She told me one about this guy who taught this reading class for these really white middle-class nerdbrats, and how every time one of them graduated or won an award or something, he'd bring the little rugrat in to see her. She said those boys had never seen pussy before, or got their dicks sucked, and they certainly never talked to no big black mama, and she had to keep such a tight hold on herself not to laugh in their scared white faces. But she sighed and told me that there was no cum in the world as sweet as a little white teen's first cum.

Candi showed me around, warned me away from the worst food, and sat next to me when we ate, to point out the troublemakers. "You stick with me, sugar," she'd say, "and you'll be outa here in six and not one motherfucking day more!" Hey, I was just fine with that. I didn't want to mess with no bad ladies.

But man, two weeks in, and I was so horny my fingers were starting to get all mushy, like dishpan hands, you know? Candi thought I was a riot, the way I jerked off every night. She said no one could give her pleasure like her old man could, so she just didn't try when they were apart. I told her that Phil was a stud, and that I was missing him so bad that I was ready to start humping the fucking toilet. The truth was, I was always a horny bitch. Since I was just a little kid, I couldn't keep my hand out of my panties. Shit, I was getting off playing boyfriends with my pillow when I was about eight or so! And I did miss Phil, kinda. Even though it was all his fucking fault I was in this to begin with.

But just because I was horny didn't mean I was asking for what happened. I mean, you have to understand that; it's just like they say at all the women's shelters. No one asks for it, and I certainly didn't. What happened was just not my fucking fault.

What happened. That's the whole fucking point of this right? OK, I'm getting to it. Weeks go by, and I'm just fine. Candi's my friend, I stay out of everyone's way, I say the right things in the support-group thing that Candi said looked good in your file. I even went to fucking church on Sundays—what a laugh, but you know, you gotta keep appearances up. I figured that by the time I was through, I was gonna look like a little choirgirl right out of the Sisters of Mercy Sunday School.

But there's always a fuckup waiting in the shadows. Just waiting for things to settle down, waiting for people to relax and think, hey, things aren't so bad. And then, wham! you get slammed real fucking good.

And none of this was my fucking fault. It was Candi's. Well, not really. I mean, she didn't ask for me to get involved.

Maybe I should tell the whole story. You see, Candi's old man had about six, seven, maybe eight girls, a real entrepreneur. And she was not his best bitch, not by a long shot. But she had class, and she had regulars, so she had steady employment. Then the asshole gets a new bitch, and she is one mean motherfucker. First, she gets him to really whack away on the girls who aren't producing like she thinks they should, and then she starts ragging on the girls who are doing righteous work. The way Candi told it, this bitch was really just interested in keeping her own butt off cheap mattresses, even if it meant that the other girls were doing $25 blowjobs in commuter cars on their way out of the city.

So, anyway, Candi gets up in this bitch's face about it, and let's just say they weren't best friends. But the next time Candi gets picked up and taken on the tour downtown, suddenly there's no lawyer and no bail. Candi's no 'burb, though; she's got her own backup, and she gets her ass out the next day. And the first thing she does is get one of her steadies to pay a visit to the bitch. Now Candi wasn't doing this to scare the bitch, but to take her out. She wanted her man to cut her, like that model in the fucking newspapers, make some really scary bitch outa her. So you can't think that Candi was all sugar and nice thoughts. But when you're a hooker, the only heart of gold you know is the one your daddy wears around his neck, the one he bought with your cunt.

And the most messed-up thing about it is that instead of hating your daddy for treating you bad, you hate his other girls.

So Candi sends out her man to cut this bitch that

made her daddy leave her dry at the tank. Got that? But the bitch got a man of her own, and the boys gotta fight, and then there's a dead guy, and then the girls gotta get in on it, and the next thing is that everyone gets hauled in on murder and assault and all kinds of really heavy shit. Candi ends up with two years on an assault charge, and the bitch ends up in the hospital with some of those cuts that actually got made before the boys got to defending the honor of their whores.

And Candi is my cellmate. And when the bitch gets out of the hospital, she gets in touch with her friends inside, and they decide to teach Candi a lesson. And when they think about it, since the bitch's man bought it, they'd take out Candi's main squeeze.

Who they thought was me.

See how this stuff gets fucked up? I mean, just because Candi never turned down a snatch shoved in her face, they think she's lesbo, and so I must be, too. Really fucking bright, right? She's not, and I'm not, but everyone's gotta assume things, make up stories to fit their ideas of what everything has to be.

They took me down after lunch, when I was supposed to be learning how to fold towels and sheets and shit. Yeah, it happened right where those shitty movies say it happens. And you know why? Because it makes sense.

You can't get into the cells when they're locked, unless you've got a few guards feeling good about you. And even then, the cameras and the sweeps will catch someone where they shouldn't be and wham! you're doing disciplinary time. You can't do it in the library—the noise would be too much. You can't do it in the fucking rec room, because there's dozens of girls around, and if one of them doesn't like watching, the guards are in and you're fucked. (That doesn't mean no one gets whacked in rec, though. I once saw a bitch take about a dozen hard belly punches in the middle of the big commercial break during the Super bowl. She was cheering for the wrong fucking team. When the guard asked her why she was puking her guts out all over the floor, she didn't say a fucking thing. One of the hard-timers said, "Bad popcorn." Not a single bitch in the room even cracked a smile.)

But in the laundry room, you got noise. Holy shit, you got noise! The washing machines, the dryers, the whole mess, is nothing but hot and wet and noisy. And even though you got guards there, the last thing they wanna do is stand around in the heat and mess, watching women dump, sort, carry, and fold. Besides, these girls had something going with the fucking guards. They had to set it up just right.

I was waiting for this girl to toss another pile of sheets in front of me. We were folding them together, see, but she kept on leaving me to go get more. I was standing between about six tables full of clean, hot sheets that smelled like some really nasty bleach. I was just minding my business. I was not looking for trouble.

But it found me, sister. In the form of three bitches from hell. I mean, every one of them was a hard-timer, and later on I found out that Rica, the leader, had fucking killed her own fucking kids. Seems that they couldn't shut up when she wanted them to be quiet. And the other two weren't exactly nuns themselves.

The three of them were the Sistahs. They weren't all black, though. Rica was some kinda mix; she spoke the lingo like a Puerto Rican, but she kept telling people she wasn't no spic. They called her Rica anyway. Her best buddy was Deshawn, who everyone called Dee, who was in for aggravated assault. You wanna know how aggravated? She had this neighbor who maybe stole some of her stash or some shit, right? So she goes over to the neighbor's house, picks up a big lamp, breaks the bulb off, and cuts the neighbor lady into little neighbor-slices. Then Dee takes out the two cats in the house, leaving chunks of kitten all over the fucking place, rips up the furniture and the curtains, and helps herself to a six-pack from the fridge on her way out.

I'd call that pretty fucking aggravated.

And then there's little Weasel. She's skinny and cute, and she's got two teeth that some weird dentist sharpened to points. The prison dicks wanted to have the motherfuckers pulled, 'cause they might constitute a weapon, but they never figured out how to do it legally. Weasel is the strangest one of the Sistahs. I mean, if you wake up one morning and there's a fresh pile of shit on the bottom of your bunk, you know it's Weasel that paid you a visit. She looks like any bitch can pick her up and break her in half; but when she fights, she moves so quick, you find your teeth living somewhere down your throat before you figure out where the little fucker went to. She's just as likely to slip you an extra cigarette as cut your good bra to pieces in front of your eyes so you have to wear one of the armor-plated fucking prison bras. She was in for a long time, something about knifing a guy in the middle of some kind of weird sex-and-drug scene, with kids and goats and crack all over the place. She liked to tell people that her mother was a priestess who could lay some serious curses on them. And then she'd flash those pointy teeth and lick them.

And the three of them took me down, hard, in between three tables of folded sheets.

I didn't even have time to yell "Shit!" I was on the

floor, with Weasel's arm around my throat and Dee's fist in my belly, and before I could even breathe again, Rica shoved a washcloth in my mouth.

"This Candi's cunt?" I heard Dee ask. You might be thinking that they had to whisper. Not on your fucking life. They had to talk real loud to hear each other over the washing machines.

I started to struggle, and shout. I thought I was saying, "No, wait! I'm not!"

I guess it sounded like a bunch of muffled whimpers. Weasel clamped down harder, screaming, "It's her! Get the fucking tape!" And they wrapped tape around my head, pushing that fucking washcloth as far as it could go in my mouth. And then Rica taped my eyes shut too. It pulled at my hair, real bad. But I wasn't worried about my fucking hair. I was worried about how I was going to fucking breathe! I mean, if I had a cold, Sister, I'd be dead. It's that simple. And every time it looked like I was struggling, Dee (I figured it was Dee) would just punch her big fat fist into my stomach. I finally gave up.

Rape is like that. I mean, it's not like that stupid joke— you don't just lay back and enjoy it, OK? But if you fight every fucking inch, all it will do for you is put you six feet under. And it was three against one. So I couldn't fight them off or even make them think it wasn't worth it. So they raped me. And more.

They had to drag me off the main floor. I ended up behind the folding tables, the ones that were already filled, and up against the back wall. We were as far away from the guards as you could get, and hidden by mountains of towels and uniforms.

They popped the buttons on the front of my dress when they pulled it off, and I could hear the little plastic knobs hitting the concrete floor. Funny how you remember things like that, isn't it? I just remember hearing the little click, click, click, and then thinking, oh no, how am I gonna get those things back on before someone notices? I shouldn't have worried.

I'm laying there in my panties and bra (one of my sneakers fell off back at the other table), with Weasel still panting in my ear and holding onto my neck, and I hear Rica.

"Your lesbo bitch messed with the wrong lady, blanca," she said, to start off. "She lost her main man, so we gonna do the same to your cunt. She gets to see you messed up, girl, messed up real bad. That way, she know what it like to not have a pretty thing to fuck with!"

"This bitch ain't pretty," Dee said. She was so close, I could smell her breath; it was like old bacon. "I bet she dyes that fucking hair."

"Let's see!" Weasel said. Her voice was high, like a squeal. I could tell she was getting excited, because every time I shifted, she just clamped down harder and giggled.

Dee was probably the one who tore my panties off. I guess she was disappointed at my red snatch. She showed it by punching me right there, right between my fucking legs.

If guys feel like I felt when they get kicked in the balls, no wonder they get so pissed. I thought I was going to die. But I was so wrong. I was so fucking wrong. That was the nicest thing they did to me.

Before I could try to kick her, she shoved a few fingers up my cunt, and the three of them laughed. Weasel (her fingers were long and bony, I could tell it was her) grabbed hold of one of my tits, keeping her arm tight around my neck, and squeezed it, hard. Her fingers felt like they were gonna break right through that tit, just burst it open like a balloon. I screamed, and I heard it all in my head, but not outside the gag.

Those fucking cunts just laughed some more. And kept right on going. With someone fucking my snatch open, I felt hands all over my body. Both of my tits were clamped down on, like someone was holding onto them like a bag caught in a subway door. I felt something cold spill on my crotch; it was this gloppy shit we used to get the really bad stains out of sheets, you know, like shit stains and blood. And Dee grunted and snuffled like the pig she was as she just started shoving this glop into me.

"We gon' get you nice and wet," she yelled at me. "Gon' get you wet for good and nasty!"

She had about three fingers in me, I guess, then four, and I started to really scream. My nose was getting clogged, and to breathe I had to snort out the snot, which was really disgusting, but what could I do? The bitches laughed again, called me names, told me I was just a little snotnose cheap *puta*, a kiddie whore, a sucker of diseased cocks. They told me I was gonna get sick, die maybe, but first I was gonna get ugly. When they started in on that shit, they began to hit me again, on my tits, on the side of my head. One of them kicked me, down at the bottom of my leg—my calf? Over and over again. It was gonna look like someone backed a fucking taxi over it by the time she was through.

And then Dee started really slamming into me, all her fingers at once. And then she started folding them up. Sister, I felt like I was giving birth. It hurt like a motherfucker! I was screaming so loud, even with the gag so tight, I just didn't know what the fuck was going on. It just felt like someone was shoving a bowling ball up my twat, and I couldn't breathe.

My sister Linelle, she gave birth once, she had this way to do it without it hurting a lot. But she said, even with all the fucking panting and blowing and relaxing and pushing, she was sweating like a fucking pig and screaming for mama, Jesus, and all the saints for hours. And she didn't have a fucking washcloth in her mouth, either.

"Ey, look! I gotta cunt on my hand!" I heard that like it came from another room; I was that far gone. It was like their bodies and their hands were all over me, but their voices were a million miles away. When Dee started slamming her fist in and out of me, that slimy glop squishing around, falling out and pooling all around my ass, and more of it being dribbled all over my crotch, I started choking. Suddenly, the hands on my tits, the pain in my leg, even the cut I could feel on one side of my head, they were all nothing. Soon even the fist in my cunt was nothing. Only one thing mattered. Air! I knew they were gonna fucking kill me, fuck me to death, make me choke to death on a fucking washcloth. Snot was just all over my face—I couldn't breathe anymore! And I started to get dizzy, and then I tried to fight them one last time.

And then, I just went limp. I couldn't do shit anymore, so I guess my body just flopped back to die.

That's when they took the gag off. They just ripped the tape away, pulling out hair and skin, and dragged the washcloth outa my mouth. My tongue felt like it was three times the normal size. I couldn't have screamed if I wanted to, but someone smacked me hard across the mouth anyway. I realized, while sweet, hot air was hitting my chest, that there wasn't anything in my cunt anymore, and I thought that maybe they were finished.

They weren't. They just turned me over, onto my hands and knees, and someone slammed my head against the floor. I ended up bent over like a Muslim guy at prayers, my ass up and my head down. My lip and my forehead were both bleeding. Something fat and cold was shoved into my snatch.

"Thas it, pipe-fuck the bitch," someone yelled. They were shoving a heavy pipe, the kind most inmates would love to keep for self-defense purposes, right into me. And sister, let me tell you, it was still nicer then Dee's fat fist, OK? But they had other things on their mind, too. Someone scooted down in front of me, and grabbed my hair. I could hear Rica's voice in my ear.

"Since you so friendly with the cunt, maybe you like mine!" And she dragged my face down into her crotch.

I keep telling you I'm not a lesbo, right? Well, that means I never ate cunt before. I used to have a trick or two that liked to do it, but mostly, it just wasn't something I got into, from either end. Like I said, I like to fuck.

But sister, I dove in like an old bulldyke on fresh bait. If it was gonna keep me alive, I was gonna do it, OK?

I never had my face in a cunt before. Rica smelled bad, real funky, like she hadn't showered last night. And you better believe that the State don't provide fucking feminine-hygiene kits to the bitches, OK? I mean, this was no springtime fresh pussy. But at least she wasn't on the rag, and if it smelled funky, it still smelled like pussy, so I just did what I guess anyone thinks you should do when you're down there. I stuck my tongue in and licked. Sister, I almost gagged to death at first, but I got used to it. I had no choice. Whenever I pulled back, she just slammed her fist into my head and pulled me into her, grinding my face into her shorthairs.

And, in the meantime, I had this pipe being

shoved in and out of my cunt, like a piston, and someone was dumping more glop on me, slathering it down my asscrack. So you know, the next thing I feel is the pipe sliding out of my cunt and into my ass.

Did I say sliding? Being shoved in is more like it. I mean, I like a nice stiff cock up the shit chute on a good day, with lots of greasy lube. But cocks got skin on them; they got fat. And they're smooth, and rounded. But a pipe is just hard, and it doesn't have a nice smooth end, and it doesn't bend and squoosh to fit in right. I was crying into Rica's snatch while her girlfriends shoved this pipe up my ass and giggled.

By the time Rica got bored, they were all ready to switch. With a few hard punches to keep me quiet, they maneuvered around me and I found myself face down in another dirty cunt. And while I ate this one out, I felt Weasel's hard, bony fingers squeezing into my pussy. Soon, she had her fist in there, and I was getting screwed every way possible. My mouth was full of cunt, my ass full of steel, and this scrawny bitch had her fucking fist in my snatch.

They kept changing places, fast, hitting me harder and harder every time they switched. Sometimes it felt like I had nothing but pussy all around me, ooze and sweat and blood and piss, until my mouth was full of this filthy soup and my ass and cunt were nothing but two huge open wounds. I began to taste the goop on their hands and their cunts, and when that became too much, I finally lost everything—I mean I upchucked my lunch all over some bitch's lap. I guess it was Weasel, really, because Dee had to pull her fingers out of my asshole to pull me back and slam my head into a table leg. They all got up then and kicked me, someone landing a really hard one just over my belly, another one right between my legs. Their expressions of disgust were mixed with more laughter as Weasel took her revenge by standing over me and pissing all over my face and tits.

And then they left.

The whole thing took less then a half hour, or so the guards swore at the hearing, because they couldn't have been away from the room longer than that. I don't know. It seemed like forever to me.

I spent four weeks in the infirmary with a cracked rib and a mild concussion and the little piece of my cunt that needed a few stitches, plus the fact that I picked up a real nasty yeast infection and then had a motherfucker of an allergic reaction to something in the laundry goop. I sang like a fucking canary, and all sorts of people were called in to testify, including Candi. At the end, I was given a month in solitary, and they shoved me outa there as soon as my first parole hearing came up. The Sistahs got a few more months added to their sentences, and Rica ended up transferred to another facility. But I wasn't gonna take no chances. When I got out, I was ready to move, sister. I wasn't gonna stay in town with the friends of these bitches waiting to take me down.

I met with my parole officer four times before I got word from my sister that she'd lend me the money to move. Phil was still in jail; and besides, he hadn't written to me once, the prick. So I headed west with nothing but my clothes and about a hundred dollars. But my cunt was all better, so traveling money wasn't a real problem. I just needed enough to put down some money on an apartment. I wasn't gonna live in the streets, that's for sure.

And that's how I ended up here, see? I mean, I didn't intend to come to this city, I was thinking I'd rather go somewhere warmer, like L.A. or something. But everyone said I had to see this city, with the hills and the pretty houses and the bay and every-

Dont Get Me Wrong

thing, so I figured what the hell? And even though there are so many queers here, there's still plenty of business for me.

And I got a boyfriend. I told you that, right? He is fine, truly fine. He looks like—what's his name, Kevin Costner—and he's got this amazing business, sending dead flowers to people. No shit, that's what he does. And he's hip to what I do for cash; it don't bother him. In fact, when we're doing the nasty, he likes me to tell him what a stud he is compared to the tricks I see, how much bigger his dick is and how much longer he lasts, and how much more interesting and talented he is. And when he fucks me, I feel like I'm goin' to heaven. And that's the truth. He is one hot stud.

But there's this thing; I'm not queer, right? And I like him a lot, and I love doing sex with him.

But goddammit, I just keep thinking about what happened in prison. I don't think about it during the day, or when I'm working. But when I'm alone and jerking off, or when I'm with my boyfriend and we're going at it like two cats in an alleyway, I keep thinking about me, on the cold concrete floor, a pipe up my ass and a fist in my cunt, and my mouth slurping all over some dirty, smelly snatch. And I cum, sister.

It's the only thing I think of when I cum.

BARBARA LOUISE

Beforre the Stonewall Rebellion, in the summer of 1965, at the age of twenty-one, Barbara Louise first entered Gay Life (such as it was) in Akron, Ohio. Twenty-five years later, she came out again, into the Leather Scene in New York City.

Meanwhile, she has been a speaker for Gay Liberation, a Pro-Choice activist, a Rape Crisis Advocate, a Take Back the Night organizer, a feminist newspaper publisher, a communal-living-experiment failure, and a lover of as many wimmin as she could get her hands on, oh yes. Although this is her first publication of erotica, she has completed a science fiction novel not yet available in print.

Approaching fifty, Barbara Louise declares that she is happier now than she has ever been in her life. She also says that she is having the most glorious and satisfying affair of her life with the sexiest and most beautiful leatherwomon in the universe.

We should all be so lucky.

LEATHER
AND STEEL

I first saw her at a meeting to organize our local Gay Pride Parade. The Facilitator was starting to read a list of possible sponsors when she looked up and said, "Oh, good, Sheila decided to come."

She banged her way through the double doors, wheeled into the room, and zipped into the circle. Sheila wasn't a cripple, she was Specially Mobilized. Her strong, active arms had intricate control of the chair. She wore black leather gloves, so tight, so form-fitting, they emphasized the long length of her bony fingers. Her face was as thin and as sharp as a hatchet, with a hawklike nose, noble and proud.

It was late March and it had been a cold spring so far, but I felt battered by my own private heat wave. I loved the shine of her classic black leather motorcycle jacket. The room was crowded, but she stood out as if she were made of neon. She was so bright, so articulate, no one noticed her legs, scrawny as pipe cleaners, and her frail body in the narrow wheelchair. I wanted to catch that skinny form in my arms and press her to me, feel her bones pressing against my chubby flesh, cushion her, hold her.

I was fascinated with every move she made, watching her hands cut the air like knives as she talked. She had several rings on her fingers and chain bracelets on her thin wrists. I wanted those hands to touch me, clutch me, hold me, and, to my surprise—since I had heard about her kinky tastes—hit me, spank me.

I attended every meeting of the Gay Pride Parade Committee, watching her, a lump in my chest rising into my throat, making my eyes water with lust for her, too afraid to speak of my desire. She volunteered for the sign-making group, so I did too.

At the first meeting, catching me unawares, Sheila came up behind me and nudged me gently on the back of the legs with the footrest of her chair. I staggered forward and fell to my knees. In that position, my face flushed with embarrassment, I turned around and looked up at her. She smiled down at me, her teeth bright and feral. As I stumbled to my feet, she said, "You've been staring at me for weeks."

"I, uh, I umm, uhh ..." My breath caught in my throat. I wanted to throw myself down on my knees again.

"You know what kind of dyke I am?" she asked.

I nodded dumbly, dizzy with embarrassment and lust. I staggered back away from her and clutched a table for support.

She moved her chair close, pinning me against the table.

I felt the heat rising from my guts, spreading through my chest, down my arms, up my neck, onto my face. "I, uh, um …" I ducked my head, took a deep breath, raised my eyes to her— (Goddess! How her eyes burned! They would bore right through me, like a laser!)–and I said, "I-find-you-very-attractive," all in a rush. Then I hung my head again and stared at my shoes that needed shining, my face hot with lust and embarrassment.

I heard the soft whirl of her chair. The footrest gently nudged my shins, and I looked at her again.

Smiling that sardonic smile, her eyes still burning a hole in my heart, she said, "Come to my house tomorrow afternoon. I will bind you with chains. I will scourge your flesh with leather. You will cry with pain, and maybe, if you take it well, I will allow you release."

I thought how I wanted her in more usual ways, how I wanted to taste her, hear her moan with pleasure. "Could I—uh—would you let me—uh—service you also—uh …"

"You will call me 'Mistress.' Is that clear?"

"Yes, uh, Mistress."

She grabbed the controls of her chair. "I'll see you tomorrow. Don't wear a bra. And I always require service from my bottoms." Her chair whirled around and left me quickly. Her voice. Our drama. I watched her go, shaking, dissolving into a pool of pure desire.

"Put your bag down right over there," Sheila said, smiling at me from her wheelchair. She was wearing black woolen trousers and a red silk shirt with black piping. I stood just inside the front door of her house. A gush of cold air from the storm outside swirled around us.

She pushed the door shut. "No. Don't take your coat off yet," she said. "Turn around. Back up a little towards my chair and straddle my feet. That's right.

Undo your belt and unzip your pants. Okay. Now bend over."

I did as she told me, resting my head on her thin black boots and bracing my hands against her immaculate green carpet, terribly conscious of my ass in the air above her lap. Sheila jerked my jeans to below my knees and then slowly, slowly pulled down my panties, emphasizing my vulnerability. Except for my naked bottom, the rest of me was still bundled up for a walk in an early-spring snowstorm.

I gasped when she quickly, possessively ran her cool, bony fingers over my curves and into the cleft.

"Open your legs a little more." Now she could see and reach my cunt. She quickly filled it with a finger, gently caressing my crack with the rest of her hand. "Been thinking about me?" she asked.

"Yes," I whispered.

"You're wet already." She reached between my legs with her other hand and tickled the hairs over my clit.

I moaned with sexual hunger.

"Why did you come here?" she asked quietly.

Ass quivering in her hands, my voice muffled against her shiny boots, I answered, "To give you my desire, my power ... and my love."

Keeping one finger in my cunt, she slapped my ass hard and snapped, "Don't mumble. Speak up."

"To give myself to you," I said, turning my head and trying to look at her.

She pulled her finger out of my cunt, and quickly backing up her chair, said, "Stand up. I'll be in the room left of the bathroom when you finish your shower."

Still in my down-filled ski jacket, with my jeans down to my ankles and my panties at my knees, I turned and watched her whirl around with a motorized hum and shoot off across her big living room. A cold draft from the door reminded me of my bare ass and wet cunt.

The room on the left, her Discipline Room, had a waxed hardwood floor. It was empty of furniture except for a three-legged stool. A chain hung down from the ceiling directly above it. Racks along the walls held whips and crops and chains and leather restraints.

Sheila was now dressed entirely in leather the color of oxblood. Not knowing what else to do, I had put on my street clothes after my shower. "Straddle the stool," she said, "with your back to the door." She zipped over to the wall in her chair, and threw a pair of black leather wrist restraints at me. "Put these on."

While I did, she loosely belted my legs to the stool with wide leather straps. "Unbutton your blouse and expose your breasts. Why are you wearing a brassiere? Take it off, throw it over in the corner, out of my way. Damn it, I told you not to wear one. Take down your pants." She then handed me an oval of metal about two inches in length, bigger at one end than the other. "Clip your restraints together and then clip them to the chain overhead."

With my arms over my head, hands drooping in the leather restraints, my legs were strapped to the stool legs while my bare ass was hanging off the edge of the stool.

She went over to the wall and took a whip with long tresses off a hook. It looked like a cat-o'-*thirty*-nine-tails.

Sheila began whipping my ass, slowly at first, softly, and I thought: this isn't anything, this is pleasant. I wished she would hit me harder, disappointed that there wasn't the thrill I thought the pain would bring.

The stinging was very bearable, radiating outward from the spot where the whip met my soft flesh.

I stood, braced on the high stool, with my pants around my ankles, and my undies around my knees, my hands in restraints stretched above my head, and my large, plump breasts hanging out of my unbuttoned shirt. Sheila began hitting me harder, and suddenly I began to worry I couldn't take the pain. I knew she would stop if I couldn't stand the whip, but I was afraid because I didn't want to be too cowardly and embarrass myself.

She stopped for a few seconds and got another whip from the rack on the wall. The next whip hurt. Each stroke etched my existence in fire. It was hard to concentrate, to force myself not to shift on the stool and hide my vulnerable ass.

Just when I thought I couldn't take any more, her wheelchair hummed as she whirled around in front of me, her smile broad and frightening. She began gently whipping my breasts. Carefully she hit first one nipple and then the other with the tip of the whip, and I jerked, pain like liquid fire running from the nipple over my whole breast.

I screamed, "Oh, Mistress, please don't! I can't take that!" but she ignored me, and since I didn't say my Safe Word, I knew I didn't want her to stop even as I cried and begged. My nipples stood out, bigger than I had ever seen them. I had just barely recovered from the pain in one breast when she would hit the other nipple.

After an eternity at my breasts, she returned to my out-thrust ass. "I don't want this to get cold," she declared. I could hear the whip cutting through the air. The slight chill of the room moved across my hot nipples. I gritted my teeth, trying not to twitch away as my ass warmed under her relentless beating.

Once again, she went around to my front, hitting the whole breast now with the thick heavy lashes of a third whip. They bounced with each stroke, emphasizing their weight, and my clit throbbed in harmony.

I began to dread the soft hum of her chair as she went to the rack on the wall and picked up whip after whip, each one harder and heavier than the last. The juices of my arousal drenched the leather seat of the stool. I was afraid I would slip off and was grateful for the wide leather straps binding my legs.

Soon the universe contracted to only my half-naked body hanging from her ceiling by my hands, my ass and my breasts exposed, all the most vulnerable parts of myself in pain, and my beloved tormentor whirling around and around me, seeming to go faster and faster, the hum of her chair mixing with the snap of the whips against my soft skin and my cries of pain and delight. Every stroke seemed to echo in my cunt, and my hunger grew until I thought I would scream with my need.

Finally, she stopped, and released my legs. "Unclip your hands from the chain. Unbind yourself. Come here."

Shaking, I clambered from the stool and stood in front of her chair.

"Flip up the footrests," she told me. "Now pick up my legs and put them over the arms of the chair." I did so. "That's it. Since I am not bleeding now, you may service me with your mouth. On your knees."

Her skinny, paralyzed legs hung over the arms of the chair. She unsnapped a leather patch over her crotch and exposed her cunt to my eager mouth. I drooled with anticipation.

"Go slowly," she told me. "Blow on it first. That's it. Now kiss it, lightly, very lightly, reverently. Okay."

The smell of her filled my nostrils. I was flattered that she was so aroused from whipping me. I could still feel the heat and the tenderness of my ass and breasts as I knelt there in front of her chair.

"Now you may lick, carefully, gently along the edges of the labia." She began whipping my back with a soft, heavy whip, calling me to my task. As if I needed reminding to do the thing I loved most in the world!

"Now, get your tongue in there and open me up. Ah, yes. Good." She tasted sweet, so sweet, in delicious contrast to the stern harshness of the whipping. The smell of her invaded me, flowing from my eager face down through my chest and belly to my cunt, and finally to my legs and toes, which twitched with pleasure.

I licked her clit, pausing to run my tongue into her cunt, and then back to her clit. I moaned. Her whip thudded against my back. I licked and licked, and her breathing changed, became ragged with pleasure. She began to tense. I became exultant, anticipating her orgasm.

Suddenly Sheila grabbed the cloth of my shirt at the shoulders and pulled me off my knees. "Come here and kiss me," she demanded. Our lips met for the first time. Her tongue thrust itself past my teeth.

She pushed me away. "Back on your knees. That's it. Yes, yes. Do it!" She whipped me harder, each stroke very accurate, even as I quickly licked her to climax and her cunt jerked and jerked with each throb of her pleasure.

"Get up," she gasped. "Stand at attention." She lolled in her chair, watching me with half-closed eyes, a superior smirk on her face.

I stood beside her, my own cunt aching unbearably with my need, waiting for the relief she had promised me, hoping I had been "good" enough.

After a while, she said, "Come here, slut."

I moved the short distance towards her on legs stiff with passion.

Quickly, she invaded my cunt with her hand, possessively digging deep, thrusting into my sex, flicking my clit hard. I moaned, and swayed on my feet. She kept this up for several minutes while I swooned with the pleasure and fought to remain standing at attention as she demanded.

"You need reminding," she growled. "Your ass is too cold. Turn around. Put your head on the seat of the stool and grab the legs."

The leather seat was damp and smelled of my juices. She used a heavy, hard whip and began flaying my ass again, with such vigor I gasped with shock. She hit me quickly, repeatedly. The pain spread from my burning behind down my quivering legs. I moaned and bit the leathery edge of the stool.

"Stick it up. Show me you want it."

Giving myself to her, overwhelmed with lust, I lifted my ass to her blows.

She cried out, "Yes, yes!"

The whip crashed down, curling into my hungry cunt, and I screamed, "Please, Mistress, please!" as she whipped me and whipped me until there was nothing in the universe but the searing pain of her whip meeting my eager flesh.

Later, as I stood beside her, sobbing, she reflectively pulled one of my sore nipples and said, "I'm tired. I've done enough for you. Straddle my foot. Press your clit against the toe of the boot. That's it. Rock yourself to orgasm."

Sheila held my arms. My flesh hot and tingling from her efforts, I gloried in the intrusive pressure of her boot against my clit. With my tear-stained face buried in her lap, I could smell the strong musk of her satisfied passion. My head spun.

"Do it, bitch," she snapped.

My cunt opened to her boot. My inner lips curled around the leather. I rocked slowly at first, running the thin, pointed toe in and out. Soon I lost control and, clutching the cold steel of her chair's wheels, the long afternoon of pain and frustrated lust suddenly erupted within me. My shameless ass, red from her beatings, pumped up and down frantically, sliding the cool leather again and again along my starving slit, driving it hard into my clit, over and over and over until I exploded, screaming, rocking the chair with my frenzy, crying with joy as I came, her soft laughter caressing my ears.

[Ed. note: Of all the stories in the collection, Louise's comes closest to having the dread "PC" label assigned to it. There is a tendency now to turn erotic stories containing characters of particular ethnic or cultural backgrounds or characters who are differently-abled into showcases for tolerance and inclusion. Well, maybe they're just lusty and lustful characters who are there to advance the plot and deliver lots of gooshy, throbbing, wonderful sex.]

C.W. REDWING

C.W. does not, C.W. emphatically states, stand for Country Western. But she doesn't say what it *does* stand for, either, so it's up to the curious to track her down and ask. C.W. has been published before, "under vastly different circumstances" (whatever that suggests), and wants the readers of this collection to know that her last name here is a pseudonym. But be on the lookout for any C.W.s appearing at bars and hot spots in Nevada, Oregon, and Texas, three states that she claims to spend all her time in. She's thirty-three years old, and an admittedly proud switch-hitter, having played top and bottom, and even spent time in a perfectly vanilla multi-partner arrangement on a communal farm. She lasted six weeks.

She says: *Not all dictionaries have this word. But you can find it if you look!*

She can only mean the title of her story.

COPROLALIA

She's such a cruel bitch, you know? Always knows what to say, that mouth ready to snap back something nasty, cut you to long red ribbons in one verbal slice.

Makes me feel like shit.

So we don't see each other for days and then weeks and then months, and then it's nothing but a phone call in the middle of the night; "I need you, hot-stuff."

So out come the gloves and the lube, the straps and the rods, the dicks and the clips, and here we go again.

There will be kisses, hot and wet and long and deep. Tongues wrestling for dominance until we both have bruised, swollen mouths and look like we've been making acquaintances with brick walls. We hurt each other orally, biting and sucking and humming and slurping, until you'd think that her nasty, filthy mouth was too sore to keep up the battle.

It's only warm up. I know that. I keep kissing her, hard, to forestall the main event. It never succeeds. She finds a way to escape my need and snaps at me.

"You're such a worthless little slut."

How common.

So it has to be followed by slaps, hard ones to hard parts of the body; shoulder, upper arm, back, upper thigh. Red marks against the flesh, punctuated by hard sounds.

The pain of the slaps makes me bite my own tongue, and her words are swift to follow.

"You're so fucking inept, I don't know why I waste my time with you."

Profanity so early?

Then she *has* missed me.

I grin, even as I flex for the next torment, the next round of words. It has to be the strap, now, doesn't it?

Heavy, rifle-shot smacks and relentless bands of pain across a moving target, because we just can't stay still in this battle. Each move is another jarring crack, and her words punctuate the thrashing.

"Coward cocksucker! Shit-licker!"

I love it when she's at a loss for words. She's done so much better in the past. I'll never forget the time she called me an *excresence*. It seemed such a nice way of saying I was a pile of shit. My cunt begins to throb in the rhythm of the strap and the words. I knew there would be a change soon.

"You putrid dog-fucker! You slurp up dog shit for the taste! Fuck—" gasp of breath—was she getting out of breath so soon?—"You bend over for dog packs! Like to howl ... howl until they cover you with their slimy dog-cum! Then you try to suck 'em off to get some more!"

Coprolalia

Very vulgar. And gross. The change would come now.

Steel bondage, always effective when someone just can't keep still, right? But first we have to wrestle, or else they're not going on. Snarls and more profanity flow between us until the steel rattles closed, and kicks have to be dodged.

"You think you're worthy of my attention, you scabrous, syphilitic moron? You're a puss-sucking two-dollar whore, a wino's three-hole masturbatory toy!"

I really hate that. Some of my best friends are sex workers. I growl a warning.

"What's your problem, pussy-for-pay? Can't admit you trade gash for cash? Or maybe you're only taking beer bottles up the ass for quarters these days?"

The ass has to be targeted in time to that, of course. Pokes, and then heavy swipes with the rod, a snappy sound of latex, a glob of cold wetness, and slam, right up the old poop-chute with some kind of rubber thingy. Accompanied by appropriate dialogue.

"You like it up the ass, don't you?—anything, anyone's fuck-stick! We can ship you to Tijuana and put you in the mule-fucking show, you're sloppy enough to take two at a time! Then you can give your famous two-bit blowjob; hell, you can take on twenty or thirty cheap tourists in your sleep!"

Get on with it girl, this is getting old. But I'm so wet, I'm so sore already. The smell of us is all perspiration and sex goo and nasty things.

An opening is made for another rubber thing, and it slides home with an ease that makes us both take a pause to breathe. It doesn't last long.

"You degenerate ... filthy ... goddamnmotherfucking ... son of a bitch, bastard, scumsucker! Slimy ... perverted cooze, pussy-whacker, feeble jerk-off ..."

Yeah, go ahead. Call me weak. Who's gonna outlast who, babe? I yowl in response to her words and motions, and she takes up the call with a series of sarcastic yelps and barks.

"That's it, little bitch ... canine cunt! Howl to the fucking moon, you inbred, asinine, fatuous fuckup, you ignorant, insipid ... brain-dead bovine!"

Now she was getting personal.

It was time to change tactics again. We are so predictable. Tits get smacked and grasped until white finger-shaped worms appear, and our tight, reddened faces are thrust up against each other, and her mouth is against my ear, telling me all the things I hate to hear.

"You deformed, fucking eyesore ... repulsive slob, you fat, ugly ... uh!"

Finally I break. I hate it when she gets around to the physical stuff.

Letting one tit go, I smash my fist into her gut, and all her venom comes out in a rush of stale air in my face. Cuffed as she is, it's no fair fight, but I'm getting mine now. I turn and shove and fill her mouth with my answer, the answer she always gets, until the only sounds she's making are grunts and moans, and the only way she can be taken is stuffed and broken and quieted at last.

When I finally finish, I push a gag into her, and leave her to watch me through angry, wet, hostile eyes. I know she's checking her vocabulary list for round two.

But how can she do better then "fatuous fuckup"?

This story is dedicated to Raelyn Gallina, who once described herself as a submissive sadist.

DEBORAH J. RUPPERT

Deborah Ruppert lives in the foothills of Oregon's Coast Range with her hunny, her child, and four cats. She is looking forward to raising goats and chickens in the future and becoming self-sufficient, although currently she makes a living as a technical writer. Once she becomes self-sufficient, she would like to write fiction and fantasy regularly, perhaps even for money. In her copious spare time, she likes to play SexMagic games; since she is bisexual and a switch, she gets to do it all.

One of the themes this short work relies upon is the shame that some men feel when they are being dominated by a woman. Contrary to the widespread theory that no woman actually does this for her own joy, or understands and likes the implied sexism of this arrangement, there are many women who really do get a kick out of tying Mr. Macho down and working him over. If it really does get in the way of your enjoyment, well, read it as if the bottom were a woman. Or just get over it.

THE BASEMENT

Consider. You are standing in a basement. In front of you, a column, rather large, perhaps 10" around. In fact, there are several columns regularly spaced through the basement; obviously they support it. The basement is finished, warm and comfortable, with thick carpet on the floor. It is very soundproofed. You know you can make as much noise as you want.

Your wrists are in wide leather straps hooked together. I secure your hands above your head to a ring there. You see me put the key on its chain back around my neck after I lock you in.

Oh, yes, this time you will see it all.

I pull a full-length mirror in front of you and just to your left and instruct you to turn your head to the left. I put a small pillow between your head and the post to cushion it. You can see your entire body, and you can see just where I will stand. You will be able to see me as I whip you, every motion, every implement. You are instructed to keep your eyes open this time. There will be no hood, no blindfold, no way to pretend it is any other than me whipping you. You wear no power suit; you have no minions to buffer you; you are not allowed to close your eyes and ignore the fact that a woman is doing this.

I put another pillow, rather larger this time and with a silk pillowcase over it, between your legs. I adjust it so it fits right into your pubis and cushions your hips from the post; your cock fits tightly against it, and you can feel the smooth sliding against the silk of your penis. Then one webbed strap around your waist and another around your knees leave you immobile. You can move only your head or your toes, and you can pump your hips in and out. That's all. I let you know that if you wiggle your head, I'll have to collar you and restrain that point, too, but I prefer not to. I prefer to have you submit.

I stand back and admire my handiwork for a while, commenting on your strong back, the line your arms make as they stretch over your head. Your ass perks right out at me, inviting my caresses. I stroke it for a while, drawing my finger up the crack and hearing you moan as I do. You always like that, don't you? For a while, I stroke your back and shoulders and tease your ass. I reach around and rub your cock against the silk pillow. Sometimes I randomly pinch here and there while I stroke so you never know what will be pleasure and what will be pain.

I pinch your left nipple hard while I work some lube just into your butt. You arch and cry, wanting more than that finger or two. I whisper, "Just wait."

Time to get to work.

I take the light cat—the stingy one—and start to gently lay strokes on your ass and the backs of your thighs. I pick up the tempo and the intensity a bit until you are trying to squirm. You notice then why I have the pillow between your legs. Every time you try to squirm away from the whip, you grind the pillow into your cock, and I hit you harder. The pain and the pleasure mingle and grow. I remind you to watch in the mirror. You may not close your eyes, no matter how good it feels, or I will need to punish that.

"Yes, Mistress," you mumble, opening your eyes very wide.

I stop, scratching your back with my fingernails, biting your neck and stroking your ass again. Suddenly two fingers, wet and slippery, plunge into you. Your eyes close with the feeling, and I slap your ass hard. "Open!" and your eyes fly open to the mirror again. I lean back and watch you watch me fucking you with my hand. Two fingers, then three pumping you. I pull out, reach over and lube up the medium plug, which already has a condom over it.

"Watch me now. I'm going to put the plug in; you are wide open and ready for it. You must keep it in from now on, until I allow you to come. If it comes out, I will punish you, and I will replace it with the large size. Is that clear?" You nod, fascinated.

I take my time getting the plug in place, pulling it in and out and making sure you are ready for all of it. It's the first time I've made you wear a plug as we work. You seem to enjoy the fullness in your ass. One day I shall have to give you to another man—or perhaps I shall fuck you myself.

I pick up the light cat again, warming up the skin that's cooled down. When your ass and thighs are pink, and you begin to squirm, I switch to the medium cat and start adding some thud to the mix. More arm, and you squirm more. You are moaning and trying to close your eyes and I remind you that you must watch and that you do not have permission to come yet.

I whip on, moving to the suede cat, very heavy and bruising. You are breathing heavily, trying hard not to close your eyes. It must hurt awfully. Your ass and thighs are red with the starts of some good bruises. You cry and move and grind and moan.

"No. Not yet." (I can read your signals and I know you are on the edge.) "Wait until I give you the word."

I take a riding crop and give you ten very quick, very hot, strokes. You are desperate to avoid them and desperate to avoid coming.

I take the dressage whip. It will welt and may cut, it is so thin and whippy. I take your face in my hands, kiss you, and say, "You may come on the second stroke and I will continue to stroke until your orgasm is done."

"Th-th-thank you, M-M-M-mistress ..."

One. *Crack!* I put everything into it and an angry red line appears midway down your buttocks. You move in agony into the pillow and I see it start.

"Now."

Two. *Crack!* Your orgasm overwhelms you and I steadily apply three more strokes, neatly lined up, before you are done.

Then I hold you from behind, gently stroke your hair and help you remember to breathe. I slide the plug out, wipe the lube off. I rub a cool cloth on your poor bottom and thighs and hold you tight. I take off the webbed belts and unlock your hands and lower you gently to the blanket that is waiting on the floor. You are sobbing and yet in heaven; I see the mingled love and fear and enlightenment in your eyes. Yes, you have given yourself to a woman, and yes, it was so very good.

KRIS MILLER AND CUBBY

Kris Miller and Cubby are the odd couple in this collection. Miller lives in Chicago with her husband, five cats, and (as she notes) a pair of little red pumps. Cubby does not have a husband (or want one) and in fact is looking forward to a relationship with a nice lesbian daddy. (Cubby also delivered a strong hint concerning her real identity in her bio. If you visit Chicago for leather events and you've ridden on a shuttle bus, you might know her.)

Together they've delivered the only intentionally amusing story in the collection. (See "sammy" for the intentionally amusing poem.) Somehow, on their first trip out, they understood that leather women don't always have to be serious. Drive on.

DDYKNWS

As I walked off the plane, I found myself enveloped in a strong bear hug.

"It's about time you got here!" she growled. "Wait until we get back to Ironrod. I'm gonna make you pay for keeping me waiting!"

"It's not my fault the plane was late," I whined.

"Do you think I care? Take a good look at these boots," she said as she grabbed my hair tightly and forced my head downward. "You are going to be developing an up-close and personal relationship with them!"

At that pronouncement, my knees turned into water. Actually, they weren't the only thing getting wet!

We headed toward the baggage claim, blithely ignoring the stares and envious glances that two women dressed in black leather vests and chaps overlaying perfectly pressed 501s always seem to attract.

I noticed that her stride was eerily silent. She caught me staring at her left hip where I had grown quite accustomed to the presence of a multitude of keys, black deerhide whip, and silver-handled dagger.

"Damn safety Nazis at security," she said by way of explanation.

I can only imagine what it took to get the stuff off her. Maybe she does want me here after all!

After the obligatory stop at the security gate, we continued to the baggage claim area. There, among the crates of oranges, golf bags, and various other pieces of luggage was my small black leather trunk. As the conveyor belt brought the trunk nearer to us, she demanded, "Did you bring what I told you to? … and *nothing* else?"

I thought guiltily of the surprise I had packed for her and replied, "Yessir. Nosir. Nothing else, Sir."

She stared through me with a look I had come to know so well, and a tremor passed through my body.

The trunk circled out of reach as neither of us made a move to get it.

"Are you planning on keeping me waiting again? Before we even get out of the airport?"

"Sorry, Sir," barely made it out of my mouth before I sprinted off to grab it.

Trunk in hand, I turned to find her standing impatiently in front of me, lead trailing from her open hand. I started babbling incoherently. "Nosir. Please, Sir. Don't, Sir," as I looked around wildly. "Please, Sir. All these people, Sir …"

"Couldn't care less," she finished as she reached for my collar and snapped the well-used lead into place.

I focused on the back of her head, desperately trying to reassure myself that these people wouldn't notice, and even if they did, I would never see any of them again.

We got to her car, a hunter-green Rolls-Royce with its "DDYKNWS" license plate. The chauffeur slipped out of the front seat and moved to open the door. Colt, tall and thin, with legs that wouldn't quit, was dressed in a Girl Scout uniform complete with lacy white ankle socks, shiny red patent leather low-heeled pumps, and a slight bulge at the crotch.

"Looking good, Colt," I tossed off.

"How many times have I told you not to speak to the staff!" Sir snapped as she gestured absently to the driver. Before I knew it, a yellow hanky was in her hands and, in very short order, stuffed into my mouth. My wrists were grabbed, the end of the lead was wrapped around them in a move rivaled only by a master of Japanese bondage, and I was tossed into the car. As I felt the familiar leather seat under my gagged and bound body, I finally relaxed. This was worth traveling cross-country for!

Sir climbed in next to me, her keys pressing heavily into my ass, and Colt started the car. We pulled away from the curb and took off for parts unknown.

Before I realized what I was doing, I found myself rubbing up against those oh-so-conveniently placed keys. Several very pleasant moments passed.

"What the fuck do you think you're doing?" was Sir's angry question. I hadn't realized she'd moved. I felt myself being pulled to a kneeling position.

"Look at me, you disobedient little slut!"

As I turned to look at her, the right side of my face exploded in a barrage of stars and pain. The handkerchief flew out of my mouth. Time slowed immediately to a crawl. In horror I watched as the hanky flew the short distance toward Sir's angry visage. As it hit her square on her perfectly formed Roman nose, time returned to normal.

"You little worthless, no-good piece of pond scum! I have never, ever, in all my years in the Scene witnessed such a blatant show of disrespect! Colt, turn this car around! We are taking this low-life submissive wannabe back to the airport!"

Colt glanced in the rearview mirror, smirked and headed for the shoulder of the road. As the car slowed, I looked up, fear blazing in my eyes. I knew mere words weren't going to get me out of this one. But perhaps my mouth still could.

Awkwardly, I rolled off the seat, landing face down on Sir's boots. Bull's-eye! My tongue snaked out and began working on that boot like my life depended on it. For all I knew, it did.

"So, you little fuckup, you think a little bootlicking is going to make me change my mind?"

I shook my head vigorously, all the while thinking, *Why not? It's always worked before.*

As gravel crunched under the tires, Colt brought the Rolls smoothly to a halt.

"Well, if you are going to attempt to appease me, you may as well do it properly. Outside!"

I held up my bound wrists in silent supplication. "Wimp!" she spat out disgustedly as she unsnapped the lead and with a flick had my wrists untied.

I barely had a chance to rub my chafed wrists before Colt whipped open the door. I could have sworn I heard those perfect red heels click three times before they came to attention. Sir stepped from the car, and I followed her hurriedly.

"Hit the car and present yourself!"

Colt carefully closed the car door and I hastened to obey, quickly moving into an exaggerated frisk position on the side of the car. I felt Colt's hands furtively cup my ass before they moved to unbuckle my chaps. With agonizing slowness, the zippers came down, and my chaps were carefully pulled away from me. The warm wet spot between my thighs quickly cooled as a breeze reached up and fondled my legs.

She grabbed the back of my shirt saying, "Okay, hotshot. I seem to remember you have a date with my boots!" She threw me to my knees.

I put out my hands to break my fall. I stifled a yelp as the small, sharp rocks cut into the palms of my hands. She leaned against the car, crossed her arms, and her gaze once again caused tremors to course through my body.

I got to work. I reached for her right boot, kissed it gently, and started carefully working the leather with my tongue. I increased the pressure as I slid around and up to her instep, pressing firmly and allowing my lips to caress their way to the tip. I shifted position, reaching my ass higher into the air as I strained to get to the back of her boots. My whole mouth never ceased to worship the leather. I grasped her ankle and slowly, carefully started to make my way up her chaps. I switched to her left leg and began going back down. My cunt strained at the seams of my jeans. My ass begged for attention. As I brought my tongue down the inside of her left boot, I felt her hand make contact with my ass. Again and again the blows came down as I tried frantically to appease her anger. Suddenly I felt the sole of her right boot pressing between my shoulder blades, effectively holding me in position. I gasped and tried to ignore the feeling that the Hoover Dam had just broken between my legs.

"That's the sorriest excuse for a bootlicking I have ever experienced!" Her words fell like hail around me as I tried not to burst into tears.

She yanked me up by my collar and shoved me toward the trunk of the car. "Maybe you'd do better sucking on something smaller!" She waved to Colt, who moved in front of me. Sir shoved me and my face got buried in Colt's crotch. Colt looked to Sir for permission and coyly began raising the uniform's A-line skirt. I found myself facing a pair of white cotton little-girl panties with little green trefoils and a very un-little-girl-like dick.

I heard the keys jangle as Sir unhooked her whip, a sound I knew all too well. I braced myself as the heavy deerhide whistled through the air, landing with a decisive *whump* as it hit my upturned ass. Another stroke landed, this one heavier than the first. Some signal got exchanged between Sir and Colt because Colt's hand snaked into the panties, pulled out a roaring hard-on and quickly covered it with a lollipop-red condom. My mouth was forced onto the head of the dick as the blows continued to rain down on my ass.

I ran my tongue around the rim of the dick and sucked furiously. I slid it farther into my mouth, making spirals with my tongue around the shaft, feeling the pressure at the back of my throat that brought me to the edge of gagging but not over. I moved my tongue back up the length, nipping gently with my teeth as I went. I moved again to gently caress the head. A particularly heavy stroke crashed down onto my ass, and I was thrown onto the full length of Colt's dick.

"Don't move," came the growled command. "Colt, you can move all you need to. I want this one to know what it means to get her face fucked."

At that, Colt let go with all the pent-up frustration accumulated on this long drive. Sir's whip never stopped, and neither did Colt's dick. Just when I thought my aching jaw and my bruised ass couldn't take any more, Colt's dick was jerked from my mouth. Sir landed one more blow and then rehooked the whip to her belt. Relieved that this cruel punishment was finally over, I started to stand up, forgetting to ask permission to do so.

"I seem to recall I gave you an order not to move, didn't I?"

"Yessir."

"Then what the hell did you move for?"

"No excuse, Sir. Please, Sir. I uh … I'm sorry, Sir. I guess I wasn't thinking, Sir."

"Thinking? Thinking!" she asked incredulously. "You weren't thinking! Obedience has nothing to do with thinking, you undisciplined little bitch! It is not something to think about; it simply is. You simply are!"

"Uh … Yessir."

"Colt, the picnic basket!" Colt slid off the trunk, tugging the skirt back into place with long, delicate fingers.

Sir said, "Please take down your trousers."

"Sir?" I replied, not quite understanding what I had just heard.

"Are you now audio-impaired as well as disobedient?"

"Sir, I uh, Sir, I uh um er, well, uh," I stuttered.

"Take down your trousers!" came the command again. As I unbuttoned my jeans, my nose started to itch. And then tickle. And with a growing sense of dread, I realized there was a sneeze knocking on my head begging to come out and play. I looked around at the surrounding countryside and noticed that we were on the edge of a field of ragweed. It was no longer one small sneeze but a whole classroom full, all begging the teacher for recess.

"Please, Sir, permission to ... achoo! Aaah-aah-uh-achoo!" A frenzy of sneezes racked my body.

"Are we quite finished?" Sir asked angrily.

"Yessir. Quite finished, Sir." But then came another series of sneezes in rapid-fire succession. As my head whipped back and forth, I felt my jeans slip from my waist to my hips. And then, with the next sneeze, they dropped to my knees. Finally, as the sneezes (and the dust) settled, so did my jeans. Around my ankles. I was mortified. There I was, tears streaming from my red, bleary eyes, snot streaming from my red, bleary nose, standing bare-ass naked on the side of a deserted road. I felt like a fool.

"Are we finished *now?*" Sir asked in a tone I didn't remember hearing before. Could it be ... repressed laughter? Nah. Sir doesn't have a sense of humor. Could it be compassion? Nah. Sir doesn't have that, either.

She gestured for another hanky. Colt put down the wicker picnic basket and handed one over. When Sir handed it to me, I noticed this one was lavender. *Just how many of these damn hankies does Colt have, anyway?* I puzzled.

"Bend over," Sir ordered. "Clean yourself up."

I went to obey, bracing my body against the firm, unyielding curves of the Rolls-Royce. I cleaned my face as best I could. Colt reappeared and gingerly took the used hanky, carefully holding it at arm's length before placing it in a Ziploc baggie and depositing it in the picnic basket.

I expected to hear the sound of Sir's whip being unhooked at any moment. Instead, I heard another sound, one not quite as familiar.

"No," I mused to myself, "she wouldn't. She couldn't. Not out here. Out in the open."

Something cold and sticky was slathered into the crack of my ass.

"I guess she would" was my last thought before I felt my ass being manipulated and latex-encased fingers slid up inside me. I felt more lube being shoved in. Then the fingers exited quickly, leaving me wide open and feeling somewhat abandoned.

"Oh, Sir," I moaned. "Oh, please Sir."

"Trying to tell me something, little girl? Did you want something?"

"Please, Sir," I croaked, my mouth suddenly dry. Sir, I ... please."

"Please what? What do you want? Tell me what you need, little girl." Sir's voice dripped with sarcasm. At this point, Sir's voice wasn't the only thing dripping.

"Water, Sir. Please, Sir. Could I have a drink of water, Sir?"

Colt stepped in quickly with a water bottle, and I greedily slurped as Sir's strong fingers reentered my ass and continued to work.

"Are you wet enough now, girl? Or is there anything else I can give you?" Sir inquired solicitously.

"Oh, yessir. Thank you, Sir. Please, Sir. Fuck me, Sir. Please, Sir ..." My voice trailed off into groans and whimpers.

"You little slut. You want Daddy's dick, don't you? You want to feel Daddy's dick, hard, just opening you up, don't you?"

At that, my knees buckled and I started to slide down the car. Thankfully, Sir's fingers were still embedded in my ass, and she simply lifted me back into position against the polished trunk. I groaned and shifted against her insistent hand.

"Are you ready now? Are you man enough to stand for this, little girl? Or do I need to bend you over the back seat?" I knew it was a rhetorical question. We weren't going anywhere.

"Please, Sir. Just fuck me, Sir," I gasped breathlessly.

Sir's fingers eased their way out of me, leaving a trail of lube and girljuice glistening down the inside of my thighs. A moment passed. And then another one. I was suddenly afraid that I wasn't going to get what I had been so afraid of getting earlier. Time continued to drag. Then I felt Sir's hand on my shoulder and Sir's dick in my ass. It moved. Slowly. It gathered momentum and I started screaming.

"Yes! Yes! Oh God! Goddess! Somebody ... Anybody! Oh, yes!"

Sir continued fucking my ass mercilessly as I started to go over the edge ...

Of the car.

As I lay there, dazed and confused, I realized that no, I wasn't man enough to stand for it after all.

Sir walked away, snorting in disgust as she tucked her dick back into her pants. I tried to crawl after her, but my jeans, still around my ankles, tripped me up and I fell face down in the sharp gravel, my hand reaching out ineffectively for her.

"Colt," Sir said with her back to me, "pick her up, clean her off, get her dressed and back in the car."

Colt scooped me up, set me gently on my feet, and reached for the baby wipes and trick towels in the picnic basket.

Five minutes later I was clean, presentable and ready to go. I had blown it (I wasn't just thinking about Colt's dick), and I knew it. I wondered somberly when the next flight home was. Sir walked past me without speaking and climbed slowly into the back seat. Her hand reached out through the still-open door and gestured for me to join her. I took a deep breath and approached that beautiful Rolls. I hoped it wouldn't be the last time I saw it. I knelt on the roadside and looked up at her, my eyes pleading.

"Permission to go into my luggage, Sir."

She waved her hand in a dismissive "I don't care what you do" gesture. I staggered back as if hit, gathered myself, and got up. Colt had my trunk out and waiting. I fished my surprise out, a foot-long box wrapped in gaudy Happy Birthday paper. I came back to the side of the car and knelt in the gravel for what I hoped would be the final time today. I held it out to her.

"Young lady," said Sir severely, "need I remind you that you were to bring only what I told you, and specifically *no* birthday presents?"

"I know, Sir. I'm sorry, Sir. I just couldn't resist, Sir," I finished helplessly.

"Must I always expect disobedience from you?"

I shrugged, temporarily at a loss for words.

She sighed. "Very well, then. Hand it over."

I held my breath as she clawed off the paper and yanked open the lid with abandon. Her hands dipped in and found a small oak box. She gently opened it and discovered a 1:24 scale model of a hunter-green Rolls Royce with a license plate that read "DDYKNWS."

"You never fail to surprise me. I would have been happy with progress from you, but this," she said, as she turned the car around in all directions making *vroom-vroom* noises, "this is perfection."

"Thank you, Sir," I said humbly, tears streaking silently down my face.

"No, little girl," she said as she gestured again to Colt. "Thank you, *Daddy,*" she corrected as she took the hunter-green hanky Colt handed her from the front seat and wiped my eyes dry. "Get in."

As I climbed in, Daddy tucked the hanky into my back pocket and said, "Home, Colt. On to Ironrod."

S. BROSA

The character and "plight" of a S.A.M.—a Smart Ass Masochist—is a continual topic of conversation among Leatherfolk. Are they the bane of the scene, or the rock upon which SM is based? (And aren't such dichotomous distinctions pointless?) S. Brosa is a pen name for a proud smart-ass-masochist.

She says: *We all know who has the real power anyway, so let's cut the crap, OK? But I'm not so willing to let* all *my tops know my reasoning. Not yet. And just for geographical reference, I am from the East Coast, but I'm not who you think I am. Really.*

SAMMY

Fuck me *joyfully*
Make me cry
Give me pleasure
'Til I sigh
Beat me senseless
Grant me pain
Make me doubt that
You are sane

Crush my nipples
Cause them hurt
Growl your fury
Call me dirt

LEATHERWOMEN

Bind my body
To my wall
Make me grovel
Down my hall

Force my head down
To your heels
Make me plead and
Offer deals

Pull my hair and
Slap my face
Clench my ribbons
Tear my lace

Hear me beg and
Hear my screams
Be the answer
To my dreams

Make me love you
Make me care
Give me power
If you dare

When I'm done and
There's no more,
On your way out
Please lock the door

DENYA CASCIO

I had the pleasure of hearing Denya Cascio read this next story aloud in a room full of sharply attentive women. My suggestion is to read it slowly to yourself or to a lover, and luxuriate in the wealth of language and the decadence of sensation it evokes. Cascio is a New Yorker who has been practicing the art of poetry for more than twenty years, and her appreciation of imagery and tempo shows. But just get on with it and read. And then, when you're finished cleaning up, come back and read what she says about writing stories like this. And be glad that Cascio is working on a whole collection of her work.

She writes: *I write these stories because I firmly believe erotica is worth writing. They are SM because that is what I dream of, what I do; the erotic experience in its most heightened and honest form. The relationship between self and the body is our primary, our first love affair. To illuminate this, to pry up and lay down on the page in all its subtlety the murmurs and reverberations, the intricate web of approach and retreat, of fear and desire, and finally the fierce drive toward union, has been a task as taxing and electrifying and as ultimately as satisfying as any I have ever undertaken.*

THE ROAR OF THE SEA

The bar was a little too high for me. I felt the thin burn of the stretch under my arms and knew I'd be sore in the morning. Wide leather cuffs went around each wrist and were buckled tight. With a sigh, I let go. It was out of my hands.

The scuff of her boot on the floor behind me riveted my attention. I was acutely aware of her presence, there where I couldn't see her. The shadow movement of her body brought the gooseflesh up as the fine hairs rose to protect me. And then, without warning, her mouth was open at the back of my neck, and I felt the familiar thrill race down me, bright as always, and into my groin.

It has never ceased to amaze me—the vulnerability my neck can arouse. The gentle touch of her fingers just there can send me spinning into helplessness faster sometimes than the back of her hand or the harsh tone in her voice that I love so. There is something primitive about that place. Something in me, very deep, that shudders and cringes and pulls away.

Her mouth was open, thorough, feeding at my neck. I lost my balance, scrabbling for a hold, and could find no leverage in my widely spread feet, only the balls of them resting on the hardwood floor. Her teeth scraped at the skin, and a sound rose from some secret place in me, rose from deep in my chest, a low and desperate sound.

Her mouth came away from my neck.

"Be still, my darling," she whispered close to my ear. I quieted, but I couldn't stop trembling. And it came to me suddenly that she knew what she was doing; that simple caress had softened me up beautifully.

She ran her hands lightly, possessively, over my taut body. Her fingertips trailed the edge of the leather at my wrists, tracing a line that continued along the undersides of my arms, down and over each rib, her hands coming to rest finally on my hips. She touched me as a blind person might, and I imagined my desire spelled out as words, raised patterns of braille that she read with sentient fingertips. It was such a small gesture, and yet it made me infinitely more aware of how little I could protect myself, of the bondage that held me accessible from all points.

Her hands tightened and she pulled me back against her, moving my hips in a small circle, grinding into me from behind. The heavy fabric of her jeans felt harsh against my unprotected skin. It seemed necessary that she was dressed and I was not, the contrast of denim to flesh heightened my awareness of nakedness just as the light touch of her hands a moment before had stressed the bondage.

I felt barriers go down in my mind, felt myself give into her a little more fully. I was repeating silently, "Yes, I'm yours. I belong to you." I chanted it like a mantra, letting the meaning sink in with each repetition. I held it to me with a kind of desperate ecstatic abandon, and yet with the thought I felt my fear double, delicious knots of terror snaking upward from my belly.

She kissed my neck again lightly, pressing the length of her body tight to me from behind. The shivering that had started deep inside me spread up and outward, ran electric over the surface of my skin, painful as fever chills, as heat lightning.

She had made me wait a long time, and already I was weak and stupid with desire. The hunger in me working like a drug, my tongue thick and heavy in my mouth, every muscle slowed and softened and indescribably pliant. Even the sunlight that fell in a great thick swath through the high window seemed to be moving slowly, like maple syrup or molasses, and the dust motes in the air where they were caught in its path appeared almost motionless, halted in their progress, as if by some miracle even the laws of the natural world had been suspended and they were fixed there forever, caught in the field of my arousal.

It seemed I had been starved for days, and now her slightest attention resonated and reverberated; was magnified in the hollow chamber of my body like the small, clear note of a violin is amplified in the wooden cavity enfolded within it—the lingering harmonic hanging on my skin long after the tone itself had faded into silence. And yet it was never enough, the craving in me only increasing. The tension was almost unbearable, and I was wholly dependent on her touch to relieve it.

She must have known this because she came around in front of me, a wicked little smile lifting the corners of her mouth, a glint in her narrow hazel eyes.

"Don't be so anxious, angel," she said. "You're going to wait a long time."

I stared hopelessly up at her, and her smile broadened infinitesimally, deepening rather than widening and digging in to the fine lines around her eyes.

"A long time," she repeated, pressing the back of her hand gently between my legs, "before that hungry little mouth is full and satisfied."

She let her hand slide up my belly until she cupped my left breast, milking it, squeezing it just a little too hard so the sensation shot through me hot and silky.

"I may not even hurt you," she continued. "I may just make you wait."

She tipped her head to one side, considering me. "How long do you think you could stand it—an hour? Two? Maybe longer. After all"—she reached up to touch the cuffs with that same maddening little smile—"you're not going anywhere."

She stepped a little to the side, careful not to brush against me when she leaned in.

"Kiss me, little one," she said.

I turned my head to her, her mouth closing over mine, and I tried to put wordlessly into the kiss all that I knew I must not speak: that I knew what she could make me feel, that I was hers without limit or boundary, that I was desperate—desperate—and still I was grateful to be here, to be hers, to be stilled, bound, helpless. There was a peculiar intimacy to the moment, to the kiss that went on and on, her tongue rolling into me, over me, familiar with every surface of my inner mouth. She kissed me as if she had me on a hook, as if she were reeling me in, as if she could draw me right out of myself and into her.

I let my head go back, let my eyes close, let the heat of the kiss take me over—tropical, verdant, wet. And in my surrender to her, suffused with a strange peace, we became one thing; our two pulses, one pulse, one beat, one tempo. All urgency fled in the face of this bond, symbiotic, perfect. Her mouth fed me all I needed, all I had ever needed, while the heat rolled slowly through me.

And yet, when her hand went almost absently to my breast, rolling the nipple between two fingers, squeezing it rhythmically, I felt my pelvis strain forward, involuntarily; my body sway toward her, striving for some further contact though I knew she was out of my reach.

She let go of me and laughed.

"My poor hungry baby," she said, brushing the side of my face with her open hand.

She left her hand to rest against my jaw, and she didn't move from where she was standing, a little to the side of me. The vision of her filled my periphery, a gorgeous danger, sinister as a spoken threat. Then gently, very gently, she turned my head away, exposing that most sensitive skin that runs along the inside of the tendon at the side of my throat.

"Don't move, little one," she whispered.

I did as she said but I stiffened, already rigid with the effort to hold myself open to her, to expose this vital spot, this softest place where the pulse beats so close to the surface that life can be taken. This is hard for me, and she knows it. Some animal memory recalls this humiliating signal of surrender (common to wolves and lions, to all the hunting animals, the carnivores), this abject display of the soft throat and underbelly that says, "I have lost. You have won. You can kill me. I will allow even that."

Her mouth pursed to a perfect O and my skin twitched where her hot breath grazed it, so much sensation in the expectation that touch itself seemed redundant.

I was breathing hard and fast through clenched teeth, dreading what was coming next. I knew she would not kill me. She would take me into her mouth, let me feel her teeth, feel the danger; she would test my determination to obey while the fear turned liquid in my belly and ran thick and free between my legs, betraying me, as always.

The anticipation was almost too much, and then her mouth closed over my neck, sucking hard at the tender flesh, her teeth a sharp solid wall to pass through. And I let myself moan because if I didn't I would surely have moved, fought, struggled—not that it would have mattered, she would only have held me more tightly, but I wanted so to be good for her—and I gave myself up to the incredible sensation of being marked.

Her mouth was so hot, the sensation unbelievably penetrating, breaking the surface as the first footstep breaks the crust of new snow. Not satisfied, it seemed, with all my heart, with all my mind, with all my strength, she pulled hard at my very soul, her mouth open on me like a leech. She bore down, her teeth bruising the skin, and I heard my voice stutter and break, a perfect reflection for the sensation which came in waves, washing over me, swelled and crested, and, as I closed my eyes, yielding finally to it, broke kaleidoscopic behind them.

I was gasping when she was finished, but I kept my face turned away until she turned it back, her hand as gentle as before, her thumb over my lips as she stepped in front of me.

"Yes," she said as she tilted my head to admire her handiwork. "Yes, I like that."

I could feel the place her mouth had been throbbing, feel the saliva drying on my skin, and I knew the mark she had made would last for days.

She stepped closer, still careful to limit her contact to the hands that held me still and her mouth when she choose to apply it. Very deliberately, with almost unbelievable care, she set about marking me with lips and teeth.

Her mouth was a fierce primitive oval as she choose one spot after another to fasten on: the side of my breast, the sensitive skin below my underarm, the hollow beneath my heart where the flesh is pulled tight across my ribs. She held me still when she had to, but for the most part I pressed myself desperately into her, held myself motionless, panted, froze. She dropped to her knees and, holding my hips tightly, she marked my belly and the hollow of my groin and even the insides of my thighs.

Behind my closed eyes an image formed. I saw my body as an elaborate network of high-tension wires, the electricity in them a sizzling blue glow in the dark circle of the firmament. And even as I watched, these straight lines began to curve, bend, warp—the very coordinates of sensation distorted. Like some false projection of cartographers, latitude and longitude leapt from their tracks, freed from all true position, wrenched off their allotted courses, all drawn together by the irresistible pull of her mouth. Closer and closer they came, fused at the last by some inherent and internal gravity, until they seemed to issue from one white-hot spot; until the source of all sensation seemed also the locus of its perception.

She would stop, release me. The lines would spring back, each to its appointed place, and I would come to myself. Return to twist against my aching wrists, to feel her hand at my hip steadying me, to hear the shift of her body as she moved to select some new spot. And then her mouth would fasten on me again, her hot wet mouth and sharp teeth, battening on my sensation like a vampire on blood. And all those glowing wires, fairy-bright in the darkness of this moonless night, would meld, fuse, join, cross, converge in the one spot where her mouth held my innermost secrets.

She rocked back on her heels when she was finished. My body was starred with the dark marks of her lips and teeth. I felt her mouth still on me in what seemed a hundred places.

I looked down to see her, her dark hair a gleaming cap. Her porcelain skin seemed poreless, pulled tight over her cheekbones, her whole sharply angled face taut and quick with excitement. She had never looked more handsome.

She was still on her knees, and even leaning away from me, she was close enough so I could feel her breath when she spoke, whisper of air across liquid heat.

"I think you're finally ready," she said.

She reached back to hold my hips, and this time the tips of her long tapered fingers rested at the inside of my hipbones. Her large hands spanned my pelvis with ease, thumbs nearly together, digging in to the flesh over my pubis. The edge of her nail was a knife as she shifted it, and in one quick movement, she peeled both thickened pubic lips up and back, pulling the hard kernel of my clitoris high onto the bone, exposing it completely. Flayed, I screamed, turned inside out. I twisted once like a landed fish, hips jerking in air.

The Roar of the Sea

And then I felt her tongue, so faint it might be a breath over the length of my exposed clitoris—the touch so light it might almost not be touch, there was no pressure in it at all, just the slow slide of sensation on the surface—delicate and exquisite—and yet my whole body responded. I felt it even into the tips of my fingers, every capillary open, every nerve alive. And then, just as lightly, with the very tip of her pointed tongue, she traced the clitoral hood, lifting it and pushing it back, leaving it to slide fully around the inner labia before returning to that same slow, weightless stroking the length of my clit as before.

Whatever inner struggle there was I lost. I fought madly to get free, to thrust myself onto her tongue, to make her go at me with more force. But her hands held me absolutely firm, and she stopped altogether.

"Be still," she said.

And it came to me with a terrible, helpless despair that she might do this for a long time.

Her tongue descended, dancing arpeggios that scaled every inch of my body, each note clearly delineated, round and smooth and certain. Like a hummingbird, she darted and skimmed, never quite landing, (mocking me, mocking, refusing and refusing) and always returning to that same long, weightless lick that ended over and over with her pointed tongue at the very tip of my distended clitoris.

My body began an involuntary jump and quiver as the hunger knotted tight between my legs. I sealed shut my lips, my hair flying as I shook my head from side to side, silently miming the no that I would not speak: I caught it in the back of my throat, trapped it against the fragile edge of my tongue, tried to swallow it whole.

The moisture seemed to pool between my legs, to bead and gather like sweet dew puddling on the backs of leaves, and drip down. I could feel its slow silver track along my thigh. The flesh was so engorged that the pressure of the blood against the skin was painful. And my clitoris felt huge, three times its normal size. It rose, sharp as a child's drawing of a mountain, from the lush vegetation that surrounded it. And, large as it was, it seemed to keep growing. Each time she touched it, it seemed to swell, to thicken and ripen, thrusting back at her, my whole body harder and more liquid.

Twice she cupped the tip of my clit between pursed lips and flicked the end of her tongue rapidly below the glans, until the orgasm welled up and my knees went to water. Then she stopped, holding me away from her—my pubic lips still pinned back, going numb under her thumbs—while my whole body flushed and my hips lifted and fell, lifted and fell. And beneath my own miserable groaning, as distant and cool as the sound of rain over wet leaves, I heard her laugh softly.

I lost all track of time, struggling vainly in her grip. Orgasm became a chimera, a will-o'-the-wisp, false as the oasis in the desert, something beautiful I had always and only imagined. Like that paradox whereby a line infinitely bisected will forever approach its goal without arriving, so she managed at every moment to bring me closer—and even closer—without release.

I was as miserable as I've ever been, pinned and helpless like a deep-sea diver immobilized under the immense, the inconceivable weight of water (how many tons per square inch). And just as he will look up from under fathoms to see the thin blue light and dancing shadows that filter down from the surface, so I would look to see her—intent as ever, her hands just as steady and as strong, her delicate, pitiless mouth returning endlessly to its self-appointed task. And I let out the wail of the damned from behind clenched teeth.

The movements of her tongue were now so small, so fine, so tiny and footless that I could barely keep track of them, a constant shifting like the flicker of sparks on the chimney flue. I was so wet as to be frictionless. I could no longer tell with any accuracy where anything was. The shrill pleasure had long since spiraled into agony and still she went on. Her touch at every moment lighter, the final necessary pressure withheld or misdirected, stolen away from me like a child's hat held just inches out of reach by the class bully.

And yet it needed no more than this, the tantalizing suggestion of satisfaction and release, as now with the barest touch of her tongue, with each dragonfly lisp—softer than the wing of the yellow butterfly—the merest brush over the surface, I would feel the first contraction of orgasm, a single hopeful spasm, the empty passage clenching uselessly on air.

Gradually I became aware that she was not actually touching me at all anymore. There was only her breath, directed in a focused or a disperse stream, and it was enough to keep me at the teetering seesaw edge of climax. Then even that was withdrawn.

The room filled with the wild, hysterical sound of my breathing. And under every breath: full-throated moans, a queer-pitched animal whine, uncertain whimpers of despair and dismay. The sounds like a counterpoint to the breath that, try as I would, I could no longer control.

And yet, as I listened, it seemed to me those sounds were like some secret language between us, like some hieroglyph as yet untranslated, an Oriental character, its mute black shape twisted sinuously into air, forming all but the words that I refused to utter. I had become a pilgrim, a petitioner, a penitent; like the beggar at the gate asking alms, upturned hands wide and open, I was speaking to her, speaking wordlessly, in the universal language of entreaty and appeal. And, as I realized what I was doing, a strange exhilaration came over me. I closed my eyes so I couldn't see her, kneeling still at my feet, and I let the sound rise and swell, let it go from me, let it form intentional as words—a plea, a shameless supplication—a cry lost in this wilderness, this foreign land into which she had brought me.

It made no difference, of course, whether I pleaded or I didn't. With the deftness of long experience, she ran her hands briefly down the insides of my legs, and fixed my feet in position by slipping thin leather bands around my ankles, the straps secured to eye-bolts in the floor.

I thought I had felt as helpless as I could, utterly at the mercy of her strong hands, but I was wrong. Something about having my feet pegged apart (my body taut and weightless now), feeling myself spread wide and knowing that she wouldn't let me come yet—not yet—made the panic flare up fresh as ever.

She stood up, and for a long moment she stayed there, looking down into my face. She seemed almost distant to me, lost into her own excitement; the light in her eyes as hot and blank as the open door of a blast furnace. Then she clicked in, seemed to come into focus inside herself, the blurred outline suddenly and miraculously clear, and she smiled at me, and kissed me once on the lips, close-mouthed but tender.

She disappeared behind me, and I heard her rustling in a drawer or a box. I tried to steady myself, even my breathing, find some hitherto-unknown pool of resource, some hidden well of strength to continue. All the small aches of my body burned bright and clear in the brief absence of her attention, and I shifted to relieve them. I altered my grip on the short chains, eased the threat of a cramp from my right foot, rested my head against my forearm. I licked at my upper lip where a thin trail of sweat had caught in the corner of my mouth, tasting the salt there, tasting also the echo of her lips on mine, tasting her.

The sounds had stopped, and she was right behind me. I could feel the electric connection between us, feel her heat, her presence beating on my back like the broad, flat light of the sun, but I couldn't guess what she was doing.

Then I felt her finger, gloved and cold with lubricant, caress my anus. Her mouth was right up against the side of my neck. I could feel her lips move against the skin.

"Don't fight, little one," she whispered. "There's nothing you can do." And her teeth sank into the muscle at the top of my shoulder as her finger slid up into me.

I was tight, but not tight enough to keep her out. The lubrication eliminated any drag or pull against the skin, and her finger slipped past the tight ring of muscle at the entrance. Immediately she started a slow probing, sliding in and almost completely out again, an easy and relentless thrust. I set my teeth against the friction, as the miserable sense of invasion became sensation, gathering first in my knees, then filling my lower belly, spreading from that one rebellious little mouth right up into my solar plexus and my chest.

I flung myself against the bonds, belly out, my body stretched tight as a sail in a full wind. With all my strength I fought the chains I knew I could not break, and in doing this I felt them as if for the first time: the four points of constraint my only reference now, cardinal points in some internal compass. I was halfway between inarticulate refusal and hoarse lust, but the heat had already begun to work on me, the small persistent violation producing a searing buzz that was pure pleasure—and that buzz seemed to focus itself in my sex; my whole vulva suddenly electric, my knees weak with wanting it, and the fierce wave of arousal was as unacceptable as the sensation itself.

One finger was quickly replaced by two, and she let go of my shoulder to put more will into her work. Her fingers began to twist and spread inside me, two fingers scissoring against me, prying me apart. Without opening my mouth I made a noise, a high-pitched whine flattened out against my upper palate—the sound of someone pushed to a last hopeless stand. And I pulled away again, unable to prevent, unable even to ease this sensation which crashed over me like waves breaking over rock, like the spray of surf in some Pacific cove, the water showing green in the shallows, plume white where the force thrust it upwards, showering over me, covering me completely, my head and shoulders lost in the tumbling foam, disappearing altogether and reemerging gasping for air.

She was patient but determined, precise as a surgeon, inexorable as rain. Every once in a while she would pull out altogether, adding lube to her fingers which were already cold, slippery as eels. And, against my will, I could feel my body yielding. It came on gradually, in short, persistent cycles, the cramping, clinging muscle easing a bare fraction of an inch at a time. I could feel it give, as a picked lock gives when the hairpin catches the final tumbler, goes over rabbit-soft, and releases with a sigh. And each time I wanted to take it back, to rail and rage, to scream defiance at her.

Rebellious, I tried to lock her out, strengthened my resolve to hold firm against hers. And all the while she continued—implacable—to pierce me, to smooth and comb the muscle, her clever fingers always finding the places that made me groan and press back into her; my will ceaselessly dissolving into the will of my body (my Judas, my betrayer). I was her vessel, her vessel to be opened and filled. And though I clung to my resistance, I could feel the locked muscle becoming soft and pliant, the inflamed ring of the anus loosen; the passage dilating, opening in the face of her diligent and assiduous assault.

And soon enough, as I knew they would be, her fingers were withdrawn, and I felt the fat, solid tip of her dildo replacing them.

"Push back against me." Her voice encouraged, demanded, hot and rough in my ear. And I was pushing back against her and crying out, "No, no, no" at the same time. And then she was in, and the air whistled through my teeth as the fat head slid through with one tearing lightning pain. The smooth, thick shaft sank as deep as it could go, easily widening me, separating the sides of the passage like a plow, making a channel for itself in the soft red folds that seemed bright as flame but hotter.

She stayed there for a moment, her body sealed against mine, while I accepted it; swollen and spitted on the hard shaft, my anus convulsing in feverish little spasms around it. Her added weight across my shoulders pulled at the cuffs on my wrists, sharpening the ache there which had long ago subsided to a dull throb. There were tears caught in the corners of my eyes that didn't fall, making the room seem to shimmer around me, to brighten and blur. And still she waited, patient as always, until all quivering had ceased, until I had relaxed around this monster inside me that seemed too large, some cruel, inhuman thing. Then she pulled back slowly, too slowly, the full length of it. The channel she had dug in me caved in, closing behind her, until just the flange of the head remained inside, holding the dildo in place.

I was panting, desperate—breathing hard in stuttering, eloquent little gasps that had a maddened, crazy sound to them. Then I felt her lips against my hair, a soft incoherent noise that might have been "please, baby, please," but wasn't, and the tenderness brought the heat up to a boiling point, a rolling boil, and took it over the edge.

She pressed back in, just as slowly and cruelly as she had dragged it out, sliding home as deep as she could go. Like an archaeologist tenderly excavating a rare and precious tomb, she recarved the tight, cramped channel that was sealed against her. Deep, deep as some unfinished hole in the ocean's bottom, deep as the infinite abyss that threatens below the bridge, as profound as that. She hit some point too intimate for violation and pressed right on past it, finding or making a void, a hole in my body that was hers alone. And I started to wail as every bit of my insides turned to water, not caring anymore if I was being good, not caring about anything except that amazing combination of burn and being filled, that absolutely particular sensation of being penetrated there.

Oh, she did it well, slow and deep. My eyes were wide open but I wasn't seeing anything really, nothing but the thick, white shaft that speared me over and over. The friction of it heating me until I had to struggle against it—had to or I might burst, not into flame but into something else just as deadly. And she kept right on doing it, rubbing at some impossible core in me, gorgeous, relentless, irresistible penetration. While the sensation just continued to surge and rise, to build on itself, in serried, stepped waves, too much and too perfect in rhythmic alternation. Until in some intoxicated mix of rebellion and surrender, I gripped down hard, locked her tight inside me with all the power of those inner muscles, and I made myself scream.

She began throwing herself against me then, slamming me, hammering me, her pelvis banging hard and urgent into my rear. I threw my head back, let my weight hang from my bound wrists, curled my upper body into a perfect arc, a half-moon, bending back until my head was resting against her shoulder, the smooth, strong muscle there supporting me. I could hear her low groans louder now, hear the grunting, guttural echo of her arousal. And then she turned into me, mouth and nose buried in the damp tangle of my hair; and her voice, when it came, was so close to my ear that it seemed to be my own. "Yes, yes, yes," she hissed, and my wailing got louder and louder.

Her hand snaked around my hip, touching me finally between my cruelly spread legs. The heel of her palm was at the top of my pubic bone, the whole open surface giving me something to press against. Her middle finger slid back and forth as I rocked into her. I was shuddering, screaming, as just that pressure made the sensation complete. The serried alternation became a perfectly straight climb, and I was rushing forward. Like a wave that retreats only to meet its own shoulder, to merge fully with it, with the next one right behind it, to join forces and continue forward without attrition or loss, the rising momentum suddenly irresistible, as perfect as rain gathering in air, as the storm before it breaks. I was racing, racing forward, and she with me. The consummate union which had been promised flawlessly achieved. The circle closing. The pattern complete and whole. The power of it—which was enough to break me—finally mine because I had ceased to resist it. And, as I felt her grind the last hard, uneven thrusts of her spending into me, I came also, seeing nothing but light, hearing nothing but the sound of my own heart pounding in my ears like the roar of the sea.

T. CASEY LIVELY

Sometimes you don't need a long story to show the joy of experimentation and discovery. Surprises—especially ones so thoughtfully planned by a scheming partner—can be the essence of a memorable scene. T. Casey Lively is perhaps best known as "Florida's First Lady of Leather," an honorary title proclaimed on her business cards. A political activist and community organizer, she also holds the title of Ms. Southeast Leather. She looks forward to settling down (someday), and adding an African Grey parrot to her household (to keep the Burmese cat and the flying squirrel company, no doubt). She drives an old sports car with faded black, red, and purple bandannas tied to the luggage rack. She writes: *You guess which side they're on!*

BUBBLES

She insisted on meeting me in LA. Said she needed to get out of the country, into the big-city lights. Said she wanted some fast-lane activities but refused to let me schedule anything specific. She didn't talk like a country girl, nor did she—as aggressive as any urbanite—act like one. Only her wardrobe gave her away. At least I could count on giving her an uptown shopping spree, but what beyond that?

She arrived late in the evening. Discreet but friendly hugs at the airport, and a distinct grope on my ass just for reassurance. Expecting to escape her muggy tropical climate, she wasn't pleased with the steamy night air. The limo's ride, however, was sufficiently cool, and soon we were in my top-floor flat. With her bags deposited where she chose, she selected the softest seat in the house and nestled into its comfort. Spreading her legs widely, she motioned for me to kneel at her feet. I hesitated. "Woman of many words," I thought sarcastically.

"Come here now!" she demanded firmly with a snap of her downwardly pointing fingers. Such a sharp contrast to the formerly endless silence, the sternness in her voice got my attention. I complied quickly and, just as quickly, found my face being pulled toward hers. My long hair gave her plenty to hold onto, and she pressed her lips hard against mine. I relaxed into her strength. Into my wanting, open mouth she whispered, "Ready to play?" I opened my eyes and willingly nodded yes.

"Good, I hear the fair's in town."

"What?" I countered in astonishment. I couldn't believe my ears. Our first night together, and she wanted to go to an overgrown carnival? Not my idea of a hot LA night. Did I miss something in Kink 101? Or maybe this was her way of easing into the fast lane. Still, there was something alluring about my new acquaintance, so I decided to humor her.

"The fair. You know, Ferris wheels, cotton candy ... Ever been?"

"No ..." my voice trailing upward.

"Well, slip into something more comfortable, and, oh yes, wear something yellow. It'll look nice against the color in your skin."

Ferris wheels, cotton candy, beverage break. Bumper cars, salted pretzels, soda break. Haunted castles, sausage dogs, and so the night went. We closed the midway and scurried away, much to my relief. Back at the ranch now (as she might say), dusty, dirty and tired, I drew her bath. My body ached for her attendance; lusty wishes distracted me.

Her entry caught me unaware. I sat on the stoop of my large garden tub and watched as she began to undress slowly. She was beautiful, a large, voluptuous china doll with fine porcelain for skin. My lusty thoughts could now take shape. She walked to the tub, put one foot in, and then withdrew.

"Take off your clothes." Her voice was deep, her tone sultry and hypnotic, her eyes fixed below my waist. I could not help complying.

She stepped closer when my hands had just slipped to the delicate row of buttons on the blouse and took my hands in hers. "Get in," she said softly, glancing toward the foaming water.

"But ... my blouse ..." I objected halfheartedly.

"That's okay. Leave it on," she said, guiding me gently into the tub.

"But ... I drew the bath for you. Won't you join me?" I coaxed, sinking into the suds.

"No thanks," she replied. "I've decided to take a shower."

"But I don't have a shower," I stupidly retorted.

"So I've noticed," she said with a growing smirk.

Then I knew. All those salty midway foods and drinks galore. She stepped into the water, kneeling with my legs tightly between hers. Leaning into my face, she began to unbutton my now-fully-soaked blouse, revealing one breast at a time, fondling, squeezing the throbbing nipples with her soapy, skillful fingers. Even in the tepid water, I could feel her steady stream. We frolicked in the bubbles, enjoying a different kind of bath. My skin began to shrivel, and I didn't even care.

Suddenly I noticed that smirk reappearing. Blowing a handful of bubbles into the air, she said, "Tomorrow let's go shopping. And, oh yes, wear something gray."

CAROL A. QUEEN

Even in the realm of SM and fetishes, human nature will give rise to a group which will insist on creating boundaries, a place where they can comfortably say, "That behavior has gone too far; it is unacceptable." Concepts like "playing on the edge" challenge the comfort of being able to label other people's behavior. And while recently that term has been applied only to situations which seem to have a disproportionate chance of producing damage or harm or even death, there are kinds of SM play which scare people so much that they are compelled to label them "not the way we do it."

Carol Queen is the kind of person and writer who doesn't allow other people to determine what she does or how she tells her stories. She is a San Francisco–based sex educator and an activist, specializing in the sexually marginalized. I have been an admirerer of Queen's for quite some time, having read some of her work in the ground-breaking anthology *Bi Any Other Name* (1991, ed. Hutchins & Kaahumanu), *Taste of Latex* magazine, *Frighten the Horses*, and *Anything that Moves*. In a collection designed to showcase new or underpublished writers, she may seem a little out of place. But the fact is, we'll be seeing a lot more from Queen, so maybe this can count as an early appearance. Now on to the hot stuff.

KNIFE

Lots more things fit in my cunt than cocks. Lots more things make me come than a tongue on my clit. Those things are nice, even wonderful. I just want to insist on the right to more. A more complicated sexuality. A more thorough sexuality. Things I have had in my cunt, in no particular chronological order or order of importance: A finger. A cock. A big, cellophane-wrapped peppermint candy cane (Merry Christmas!). A hairbrush handle (my dad's). A vibrator. A toothbrush handle (more, please). Two fingers. Three fingers. Four. Someone else's. A dildo (girl cock). A bedpost. A fist. A dog's dick. A string of pearls. (I've had many of these things in my asshole, too.)

Things that have made me come, also in no particular order: My hand. Someone else's hand. Being fucked. Being fucked in the ass. Having my tits sucked just right. Being kissed while I'm being fucked. Dirty words. Breathing rhythmically. A vibrator. Being told I have to. Being spanked. Gazing into someone's eyes. Having sex in dreams. Being pissed on. Being threatened. I had already had a lot of things in my cunt before I had a knife blade slid inside, juicy and trembling. Many things had already made me come before the time a knife was put to my throat and the sear of the steely blade sent me into involuntary, thrilling, terrifying spasms. A switchblade, clicking erect at the speed of sound. Nothing is more arresting. I don't even need to see the knife to know what comes next, to get wet and weak-kneed, to feel ready to give over. My breath stops for a minute and I am light-headed from fear and from this incomprehensible welling-up of desire. I was always afraid of knives. I was afraid of men with knives. Afraid of men with knives stalking me, men with knives who wouldn't be done 'til they'd cut some part of me away. Now I think about all the newspaper stories which wouldn't quite say what the men with knives did, how before I knew about getting turned on I knew about the titillation of horror, how before I knew I was getting turned on I was being set to wonder about, obsess about, dream about, pulse racing and breath cut short, men with knives. I was a little afraid of women with knives, too, but it didn't mean the same thing. Women with knives were sexy and stronger than me. Women with knives could protect themselves. I would be safe at the side of a woman with a knife, and before she turned her strength to me, she would put the knife away. When I caught myself wishing she would bring the knife to bed, would stroke me with the steel, would show me all her strength, I was afraid, but I stopped having nightmares about men with knives.

Knife

The steel is cold, but my skin tempers it and makes it warm. Why do they try to terrify us, why do they want us to think we are weak and in danger? Someone wanted me to be afraid of knives. Someone wants me to feel powerless. I do not know why the unexplained alchemy of my subconscious, with pots of mystery juice roiling in my cunt and heart and brain, has taken things I was afraid of and turned them into sex. But I do know about the power of my skin to warm a knife blade. I know it smells powerful when I lick the knife's flat side and taste pussy and heated metal. I know something no woman is supposed to know: that when I want to have sex, I can have it with anything. My lover is a man with a knife. What does it mean to fear someone I trust? Is it possible to trust someone that I fear? I open the door to his knock and he slips inside, gets me by the hair, pulls the knife. I hear it click and it strokes my throat: "Scream and I'll cut you," he says, and he is using a very different voice than he uses when he says, "I love you." This is everything I was too terrified to imagine. This is how the men in the newspapers act. This is worth an hour of foreplay. He forces me back towards the bed. My mind is blank, responding to the intended terror. It is simultaneously teeming, a thousand thoughts in succession, and I wonder if I were really in danger I would be thinking so hard and so fast, and then I wonder if perhaps I really am in danger; do I know him enough to be sure he isn't crazy? Did I choose a killer, a rapist, a madman? Will he stop at my demand—or if I beg? It doesn't matter, because without these thoughts the scene would be incomplete, imperfect. I might as well be wondering whether I would ever tell him to stop, because this is so good I am almost prepared to be his karmic bride, swoon as he plunges the knife between my ribs, fucks my feebly beating heart. The blade becomes the Excalibur of Romance, and we are legendary lovers, and he hasn't even backed me all the way to the bed yet. This is the litmus: that every shred of me wants him to take me, and the shame that wells up in me over breaking feminist commandments is only making me hotter. In these moments if I could not trust that the wisdom of my cunt transcends all political cant I would fly helplessly insane. He does not wait to shove me until my calves touch the mattress, and so I fall without being sure the bed is there to catch me. He is on me the second I land. The blade is with him, at my throat, and he's telling me not to scream, not to whisper, not even—to move. I try to beam assurance to him through my eyes that I will not talk or struggle, and he moves to stroke the blade against my cheeks with crazy, tender menace as I silently entreat him that I'll be good, I am going to do everything he tells me. He reads that message and brings the blade to my lips, "Kiss it!" he says, voice almost a snarl. I don't think a real rapist would do that, and anyway, that's our ritual—he makes me kiss everything he uses to hurt me. He is not hurting me with this knife. He's going to do that with his cock, spear me with it, shove it so deep into my cunt that I feel the buttons of his Levi's bruise my pubic bone; no lube, not even spit. He's thrown my skirt up over my eyes so I can't see it coming, I only know from the change in pressure of his thighs pinning mine to the bed, spreading me wide for it, blind and open and helpless and the knife is still somewhere close.

One long shove, hard. His knife, his cold voice, fear mixed with trust have made me too wet for pain, even though it was supposed to hurt. He grabs the front of my dress like pony reins and rides, rides hard. He can't fuck me hard enough. I am subatomic

Knife

with it, but the knife blade is still on me, and I can feel it trying to pierce my skin; only if I'm completely still can I escape it, or postpone it. Coming, done in silence, completely still, at knifepoint, feels like a lobotomy, feels like a galaxy exploding. The only part of my body not frozen is my cunt, seizing and spasming on his pounding cock. This really feels like I am going to die, for as long as the orgasm lasts. Of course this makes the orgasm especially precious, especially strong; and by the time I am out the other side, I have lost track of when and how it started. That I could stay still during the come was a test, and now I will find out what the knife is for. He blindfolds me with my dress again. He pulls out with a terse "Don't move, don't speak, I'm not finished with you," and I lie so still I hear my blood pound. He is tying my hands. He is spreading my legs again, even wider now: I love this, this being captured, taken. He is slipping the knife down, down my belly, over the mound, shaving it over my clit, the point up under the clit hood, and nuzzling it between my cunt-lips. "Don't move," he says. "Don't move." He's not finished with me, he says, and his hands rough on me make my skin effervesce, I hope he's never done with me; everyday awareness is such a weak shadow of this chain of moments that I would be happy to be bound up in it forever. I know he is about to fuck me with the knife. It is not about submission now. It will require all our control, each of us. Only powerful women fuck knives. We have done this before. One night at a party I was chained to a wall, my clothes ripped and cut off my body, and he was stroking my hot, alive skin with the chill steel of the knife. My cunt was running slick with the preternatural desire and with menstrual blood, so open that when he slid the blade inside my body I sheathed it almost without contacting the steel with my cunt-walls. My blood ran down the knife, onto his gloved hand, and the people surrounding us were aghast, convinced I was cut, but they saw what they wanted to see. They should have known women bleed without cutting, and the just-removed tampon was at my feet. Today we have no audience. That night we had to protect ourselves from the force of other people's vision weighing on us, making his hands shake and my legs unsteady, by gazing into each other's eyes and making each other the only ones in the room. Today we are the only ones in the room, but our eyes connect anyway—he's removed my blindfold again—and the high edge of rape energy is too puny to support what we're going to do now. "Be still, love," he says, in the voice he uses when the surfaces of our two skins start to melt together. I feel my lips spread, I feel steel against my labia, and he takes forever and ever to slide the switchblade in. I stay still, caught like a doe on the highway impaled by car headlights. But my molecules are racing, bumping each other in an infinitesimal, crazy dance, and suddenly I can feel them careening. Knife tantra. In my cunt or on my flesh, my terror turned to lust changes to pure energy. When the blade is in me I have to lie frozen, all motion in breath and heartbeat. But when he draws the blade out, the instant my flesh is safe from its sharp danger, everything that was still begins to move, to roll like waves rolling in, to writhe in the bonds like a noosed animal, an orgasm that invites in all the universe's motion now that I am released from this stillness. My voice moves, too, throat open, done with the game of silence. Of course when he is ready to slide the knife back in, the motion snaps back to stillness. Our eyes are locked again. His free hand is splayed on my belly, holding me down and reassuring

Knife

me, feeling my heart pump as he proves to me that death can fuck gently. We can keep this up all day, this slow oscillation between the two states: swimming in orgone, letting lifewaves take over my body, my being; and the vivid dormancy enforced by the knife. Later he will hand the knife to me, lie still as marble save for his indrawn breath as I learn its heft and puissance myself, trace its sharp point across the pulse in his neck. The fear in his eyes is involuntary, but he lies beneath the blade quite willingly. Letting sex take us over protects us from some of the terror, I think. I watch it in his eyes, pulsing desire that I never take the blade away.

LADY SARA

This piece is actually the first part of a five-part series which was written for an electronic audience. The author's name is Lady Sara online; in this context, it will serve as her pen name. Otherwise, the women who read it from a computer screen will think I stole it.

Lady Sara introduced each part of this unfinished work with a warning, because she wasn't sure if everyone reading it would be SM-positive, or gender-play-positive. The warning read: *This story contains graphic descriptions of intense sadomasochism, politically incorrect role-playing, and a strong suggestion of (if not actual) sexual interaction between women and men. Things are not always as they seem, and some characters are portrayed as they see themselves, not as the world sees them. A lot of the story is true. Some of it, I just wish were true.*

Well, I wish I had the next couple of parts. Maybe for *Leatherwomen II*?

THE TRIANGLE

Act One

When I saw Surrender enter the room, two slaves in tow, I almost lost my grip on Suzie's clit.

A half-gallon of Probe covering my hand and wrist had made it hard enough to frig her the way she liked it without slipping steadily into her steaming cunt. But if I wanted to get her off (and I did), I had to use less fist and more finger action. She sensed my hesitation and growled across at me, shaking her hair and straining against the two dykes holding her down.

"Fuck me, Kris! Fuck me! Please!!"

At that lovely refrain, I regathered my concentration and jammed my fingers on either side of her clit. Determined not to let Surrender make me fail, I twisted that exposed little bundle of nerves until Suzie's growls became pants, and her lovely tits began to rise faster and harsher. "Come on, Suzie girl, come on, *bitch*...." (At that magic word, she hissed and thrust her hips up so hard I felt a crack in one of my knuckles.) Since that charming upward thrust was her signal, I gently eased my fist inside her, twisting my thumb up to catch her g-spot. Her buddies leaned forward, knowing what they would see in a moment, and I leaned into her, urging her onward, pumping, thrusting....

"Oh, god, oh Jesus ... Kris, oh godohgodohgod ... yes! Yes! Ah! Yes!!"

Her body convulsed, her cunt grabbed my hand up to the wrist, and as her first orgasm brought out a sweet gush of cum, I quickly pressed my free hand down over her pubic hair and jammed her G. In an instant, my hand was out, and her startling, wonderful ejaculation began. One of her friends eagerly put her own hand out to catch some and brought it up to Suzie's mouth to taste. She was still out of it, though, leaning back, her body covered in sweat, her breath coming in lusty gasps. She bucked and writhed in continued reflex, working out all her magnificent erotic energy.

I leaned back, eased my stiffening hand out of her and stripped my glove off, tossing it to one of the attendants to throw away. Someone pressed a bottle of water in my hand, and as I was too out of breath myself to drink, I poured some of it into my hand and splashed it on my face. The next move was to splash some on Suzie's cunt—"That oughta cool you off, bitch!"—and then carefully pour some of it into her mouth.

She drank, sputtering, and then sat up. "Oh, Kris, that was *so* hot...." Her voice was hoarse, her face flushed.

"Who said you could talk, slut?" demanded her

right-hand buddy. (It seemed that she was top tonight.) Suzie grinned for a moment and ducked the light slap that caught the edge of her cheek, but meekly submitted to being recollared and roughly, beautifully, and very sloppily kissed by her left-hand buddy. Right Hand turned to me and said, simply, "Thanks," and then turned to continue the assault on lucky Suzie.

My part of their scene over, I turned away to finally take a drink, and then remembered that Surrender was there.

She was standing not far from me now, with one of her slaves kneeling at her feet, the other passing her a drink. I hadn't seen her in months, and at least one of those slaves was new. I remembered that she had known about my Contract to Sir ... and I felt amazingly conscious about the collar I wore. The last time I had seen her, I had two slaves of my own. Now ... I was unattended. Doing scenes with other people's bottoms. Attending Sir.

She was watching me. I poured some more water over my hand, to take away the residue of powder the rubber glove had left, and wiped my palm against the portion of my jeans not covered by my chaps. I really didn't know what I was going to say when I walked over to her, but if nothing else, my service to Sir demands that I am well mannered.

She was tall, elegant, and slinky in her black ciré body stocking, her very black hair cut ragged and almost punkish, her long fingernails a stunning red. Her eyes bored into me for a moment, taking in my clothes, lingering on the collar, and the keys dangling right. She was at least twenty years older then me, or so they said.

"Well, well, Kris ... this is a new look for you. I heard we are a ... boy now."

Every note ... every tightly clipped word ... stung. She really spoke that way, slowly and with great drama. It suited her. I smiled to cover my anger, and said, "I don't know about *you*, Surrender, but yeah, these days I'm Sir's boy. How have you been?"

"Fab-ulous, Kris ... just wonderful ... and, I must say, the collar suits you."

Unwillingly, I blushed. "Thank you."

"But then, I always said that a collar would suit you, my dear." She took a drink and passed her glass down to the slave at her feet. I didn't fall for that trick, which would have had me bow my head to her. Instead, I took a long swig of what was left of my water and widened my stance.

"This collar does." I said firmly, genuinely smiling for the first time. "So, Surrender, what have you been doing?"

The standing slave lit her a cigarette. "Oh, the usual. Work has been steady, slaves come and go.... I heard that you lost yours, by the way."

"They were never really my slaves."

She nodded slowly, "Hm. Yes, of course. So ... what is it like being a boy?"

It's miraculous, I wanted to say. I'm living in a state of ecstasy. But instead, I said, "It's been a learning experience. I find it rewarding."

"Hm, yes. And what exactly is the difference between a boy and a slave?" Sting. Sting.

"Boys grow up." I snapped back.

"To become ...?"

"Daddies."

"And is that what you want to be? A daddy? Going to look for your own prepubescent adjunct?"

"I'll have a boy of my own one day." I said, feeling tension make its way into my shoulders. "Anyway, it's nice to see you, Surrender." Bitch, bitch, bitch, I added mentally. I turned to go but was stopped by her voice.

"How interesting.... Do you know, my new slave has been asking about daddies and boys."

I quickly glanced to her side, but the woman there was neither daddy nor boy, clad in a lacy corset and frilly topped stockings. Then, my eyes finally fell on the creature at Surrender's feet, kneeling next to the woman's very pointy-toed black boots.

Ah yes, here *was* a boy ... soft, elfin face turned up, hair too long, but that classic "lost" expression on a face that screamed jailbait, although he was surely twenty. Surrender had dressed the little one in a brief latex bodysuit, and a stiff collar with a leash. Didn't suit him at all. In a second, I had dressed him in chaps and vest, little bulge covered by a leather jock, like mine, but without the studs.

"Jazz, say hello to Kris. Kris used to be a Mistress ... now she's a boy."

Yeah, just spell it out, you prick-licking slut, I cheerfully noted. Like no one's ever gotten a piece of *your* ass, right? But actually, I was just too charmed by this vision of adolescence crouched at her feet to wish her real malicious thoughts.

"Hello, Mistress." The boy said, unsure. Surrender's crop came sailing down across the boy's shoulders, and he whimpered. I felt a nudging of my own desire for this "Jazz" and knew that I had just lost the battle to be disinterested.

"I said she *was* a Mistress, Jazz. Address her properly."

Jazz looked up at her, obviously at a loss for what to call me. Then, after meeting my eyes and tracing a glance down to the front of my jeans, where a wet handprint outlined a distinct bulge, Jazz said meekly, "Hello, sir."

Music, I tell you. If Spike could have gotten any harder, he would have. Even so, I felt a small and sudden surge of moisture between my legs. I smiled.

"Nicely trained," I said, deflecting whatever cutting remark Surrender was going to make. "You could make a good boy out of him. Good luck."

"I don't make boys, I make slaves." Surrender hissed. "And yes, Jazz is promising. Would you like a piece of this miserable untrained slut? As a 'Daddy in Training'?"

I looked directly into her eyes and tried to sound disinterested. "Sure. When and where?"

"Next Friday ... here. But there is a condition."

I waited. She gritted her teeth for a moment and then smiled sweetly. "I get a piece of you first."

I thumbed my collar proudly. "Sorry, Surrender, but this says otherwise."

"That's not what I hear, Kris ... I heard that your ... Daddy ... lets you have your nights out of the house, as it were." She smiled again, and stubbed out the last of her cigarette into an ashtray brought by her female slave. Her information was correct, but it was *not* common knowledge. That she heard it was disturbing enough. That she said it out loud where people could overhear it from her was inexcusable.

"You heard wrong." I said simply.

"Hm. Well, too bad, then. I must be going. Good to see you, dear. Tell Sir I said hello." With a curt nod, I turned away first, in a movement that caused my keys to bang loudly against my hip. I really should have left, but morbid curiosity and the desire to see whether Surrender would actually play with her new toy made me track down a cold bottle of beer instead. Sometime around 3:00 or so, I did see Jazz, handcuffed to a suspension bar, the latex replaced by sweat and crop marks, a pale, nude little crotch devoid of that which would have marked his adulthood. His underage appearance was far too overpowering. Far from being turned on by the scene, I felt like I was watching a Thoroughbred lashed into wagon tracings. Surrender was a tough top—she always had been. But then, so was I.

I left my unfinished beer on a table and finally tore myself away, into the chill night air, and homeward. Once home, I tore my own clothing off, with snaps and buckles giving way under my fingers. Carefully, the collar went to its place by the bed, as the chaps, jeans, T-shirt and vest were casually crumpled on the floor, next to my scuffed boots. I had a sudden, harsh vision of Jazz applying hot tongue to those boots and wrapped my fist around Spike, jamming him against my clit. Still imagining the boy at my feet, I spat into my palm and began to stroke myself, spreading my legs wider ... yes, boy, that's it, lap that leather, bend that pretty back, let me see that nice, soft ass raised up to me....

I switched off, left hand on Spike, right hand nudging its way under the harness to get the fingers to my clit. Standing by my bed, I smelled my own sweat and arousal and remembered the feel of a heavy tongue over my boots ... it had been so long.... If only I had a boy, someone to serve and arouse ... to amuse and test me ... someone I could train, and cherish ... who would take my pain and give me pleasure....

My clit jumped up at the image, and I deliberately slowed my fingers, trying to prolong it, my hips thrusting forward, yes, the boots, and then up my legs, licking the leather, and then teeth and fingers hot against my crotch ... get it out, boy, get your mouth on me, let Kris fuck you, yes, so hot and tight, so good, his breath against me, his nose jammed up in my short hairs, Spike doing his job and grinding into me *so* nice, I just grab his hair and thrust against him, into him, and I feel him suddenly relax under me, taking it like such a good boy ... my boy...gonna fuck you now, boy, take me, take me, nice and *hard*, nice and *fast* ... feeling his hands creep up against my hips, clutching the leather holding on ... little, muffled whimpers, pleading me, thanking me, until at last I feel it coming, I feel myself exploding ... oh, yeah, that's it ... oh, yeah ... so hot ...

... Without thinking, I collapse onto my bed, fingering the buckles of my harness, and letting the rig drop. I am soaked, drenched in my own sweat, and the wetness between my legs is like a small river, I am so open, so wet.... I press a pillow between my legs, still thinking of his too-long hair, thinking of his face pressing against my cunt, his tongue eagerly taking my cum, and I hear him, clearly, saying, "Thank you, Daddy ... oh, Daddy ..."

I fall asleep and dream of nothing.

Act Two

Two days later.

I have stripped down to jockstrap and singlet, both white, the collar stark black against my throat, and the script is set for a good flogging, some j/o, and then maybe I get to practice my own oral skills on Sir ... but I just can't relax my shoulders. I feel Sir's hands push aside the singlet and knead into my back, and I bend my head forward to try and relax. Nothing worse then taking a flogging on a tense shoulder. But I can't, and the hiss of frustration when I begin to apologize is real.

Sir stops me with a firm "shhh" and continues to

The Triangle

work my back and shoulders. Anyone capable of putting the kinks in their bottoms should be able to get them out, I always say ... and as that phrase runs through my head, my shoulders drop just a little.

"So? What is this? Tell me."

I take a deep breath, trying not to fight the fingers working on my neck. "I saw ... a boy. I think I want him."

Fingers switched off to palms, against my muscles. "That alone shouldn't be so much of a problem. I think you should have one."

"I—I know, Sir." Turning my head, I gently kissed a hand that had slipped up on my shoulder. "But he belongs to Surrender."

"I hadn't realized that Surrender was doing boys."

"She's not."

"Ah. Relax ... you're fighting me. If the boy isn't free, there's nothing you can do about it. Perhaps Surrender can be persuaded to share him."

"She will ... if I bottom to her first."

The hands paused for a moment. "You once told me that Surrender is a brutal top."

"I can take her."

"That wasn't my implied question. I know you can take her. But do you want to? Is this boy worth so much?"

My guts churned ... yes, I wanted to say, but maybe not ... young, untrained, scared, not sure of what he wants, and after all this time to bottom to *her,* when I swore she would never get a piece of me ...

"I see that you think he is." Sir's hand slapped heavily against my shoulder, almost pushing me forward. "Listen carefully. Pursue this if you must, and get this matter done with. I will not tolerate your concern over this to interfere with the two of us, not in thought or in my access to your body. In the meantime, I want you to relax ... you're my boy, tonight, and for the rest of your contract. Isn't that right? *My boy.*"

With a sudden ferocity, Sir swept me backward in a strong, locking embrace that made my mind and crotch flood with warmth. "Yes, Sir," I groaned, in a whisper, "I'm your boy ... please ... please ..."

"Say it...."

"Oh, Daddy, please, use your boy ... fuck me, Sir, please...." Finally, I surrendered to Sir, my body relaxing, my mind totally fixed on what we were about to do. I felt the coldness of the knife cut through the singlet, braced my legs apart, and heard the whistle of a cat cutting past my right ear. Already flushed, I bowed my head and rounded my shoulders, and felt the first splat of leather against my back.

"Oh, you'll get fucked, boy ... Daddy's gonna do you *good* tonight ... brave, tough little boy, aren't you?"

Splat ... harder, the lash leaving a trail of abrasion pain behind it, the initial "thump" almost forgotten by the time the next lash fell. In my mind, I shout it, but my voice comes out a whisper again, "Yes, Sir, thank you, Sir...," the first of many litanies I will chant tonight. The lash falls faster, and I mentally count, 7, 8, 9 ... then lower on my back, lighter for a while, and back to my shoulders, where I can take the most, 18, 19, 20 ... The concentration on my left shoulder, to bring up the tracings of a cutting waiting to be refreshed ... 22, 23, ... 24! Which finally tears a mental scream from me, a physical sound that is a cross between a whimper and a harsh cry, and Sir's lips on that special spot, over the initial I had placed there, and Sir's hand reaching between my legs to find me both hard and wet ...

The Triangle

"Oh yeah ... this boy is going to get a nice fuck tonight ... so brave ..."

But I know it'll be a while before I get *that* treat. I bend forward slowly as Sir pulls the worn leather belt through the loops. First ... oh, and always ... I will take the pain/pleasure of leather on my ass ... and when the glow from the skin is as hot as my throbbing, aching clit, I will beg ... oh, yes, I will beg ... and I will cum ... and cum ... and cum.... The first touch of Sir's hand against my ass is soft and sensual, a cupping grip on one cheek, a trail of fingers tracing where the first blow will land.

I never get enough of Sir's hands ... the first blow of palm against ass is always good enough to send me into arousal. Sir has taught me everything I know about spankings ... and I give *nice* ones ... each time, hoping I get reactions not unlike the ones I make. The first dozen are light for me, almost teasing, and I press against my top, loving the teasing, wanting it harder, but not wanting it to stop. As the open-hand slaps increase in strength, I feel a hand rest on my lower back, steadying me, and I reach for the leg tucked so nicely against the front of my body. "That's it, boy, hold onto that leg ... good boy ... obedient boy...." And the force of the blows increases again, making me alternately moan and whimper and gasp, picturing the sweep of the arm that brings that loving hand hard against my ass. Again and again, the blows land where I love them, right at the curve of the ass, and then in the sweet spot, sending delicious tremors through my sex, making Spike inch his way from behind the white cotton. I clutch Sir's leg and take it all, the thumping finally setting up the rhythm that will take me to orgasm, and my breath starts to come in longer gasps, my legs tremble under my own discipline, trying to hold steady, and sweat

And then Sir stops and steps away.

Sir knows me *very* well.

By the time the strap falls on my ass, I have lost the drive to orgasm and am ready for pain again. Needing support, I am moved to lean against a worktable, and, thus braced, I welcome the slap of leather against me; I embrace the power, strength, and passion behind it. I hear a soft murmur of approval, and I am taken to a place where simple arousal has little meaning. By the time Sir tosses the strap aside, I am ready, open and hot for Sir's pleasure ... and I arch my back to make it easy, I reach behind myself to open myself, flushing with near-shame, and I feel the teasing touch of Sir's near-penetration.

"Good little boy, aren't you?" is the growl I hear behind me. I moan, my ass feeling as hot as a sun-baked fender, my fingers feeling my own wetness, my little cock pressed up against my belly.

"Yes, Sir, your good boy, please Sir, please ..."

"Look at you, little *punk*, with your ass in the air, just begging for Daddy's cock, aren't you?"

At *my* magic word, I saw stars, and almost lost a grip on myself. My pleas were buried, incoherent, as Sir pressed into me, slowly, and I forgot how to breathe.

"Soon Daddy's boy may have a boy of his own, hmmm? Your own boyhole to use?" At the final word, Sir thrust all the way into me; and without warning, I came, my body held tight up against the table, I gushed, all over my trapped prick, I spasmed around Sir's own cock, and I cried out, breathless and harsh, "Yes, Daddy, yes ... oh, Daddy ... fuck me ... your boy...."

It was the first of many.

I decided that nothing was going to stop me from getting my own boy. And making him scream with pleasure, just like I did. Surrender was going to get a call from me the next day.

Act Three

"No corsets."

"My dear, even my *real* boys wear what I direct them to." Over the phone, Surrender's voice had that edge of bitterness, a grating quality that seemed like the grit left in your mouth after a dentist takes a mold of your teeth.

"But I'm not *your* boy, Surrender. You want me to bottom or not?" Stressing the word the same way she whined to me, I waited for her to argue, since that would give me the upper hand again. But, as usual, she was quick to spot obvious tricks.

"Any *other* guidelines, my dear?" Sweet, patient, yet oh-so-biting.

"I don't get fucked."

"Kris, dear, that is your *least* worry with me. I will see you tomorrow at eight then ... you know where I am." Click.

At eight sharp, I and my libido arrived at Surrender's town house door, my back stiff from fortitude and my brain nulled into obedience by several extra-strength Excedrins. All day, I had wondered if I had finally crossed the bridge into the state of confusion.... Was I really bottoming to a woman I had seen leave a cute TV in reverse suspension for thirty minutes while she gossiped and laughed less than fifteen feet away? Was I really doing this for the promise of getting a piece of what was obviously a novice SM bottom who didn't know whether to look for a mistress or a daddy? And was I really sure that I could somehow even get the point across to this angel, this Jazz, that I was interested?

And would Jazz care?

These were all damn good questions. I rang her bell.

A woman wearing a stiff leather collar, matching cuffs on wrists and ankles, and what appeared to be a chastity belt, opened the door for me. Wordlessly, she turned her back and said, "Follow me."

"You're very rude," I said back, not moving and leaving the door wide open. "Do you always treat guests like that?"

She turned back, aware that I was not behind her and that the door was very, very open, and she was very, very undressed.

"Close the door! Some one might see——" She reached for the handle, but I kicked my boot out and wedged the door open. She reached up to cover her nice tits as she struggled with the door one-handed, and I smiled.

"Not until you apologize and invite me in politely."

"Oh, god...!" She glanced behind her, tried to scrunch her body directly in front of mine. (Difficult to do. She was a head taller then me in her stocking feet ... and the four-inch heels made matters worse.)

"I'm sorry! I'm sorry! Please come in now! And close the door, *please?*"

I stepped in, and casually kicked the door shut. "That's better. See where good manners will get you? I'll see Surrender now."

I felt much better.

Surrender's dungeon was in her basement, and I already knew that it was nice. Many people, tops and bottoms, had told me about her suspension rig, her sling, her stocks and her rack, her bench and her infamous chair, and of course I knew she had one of the largest collections of toys I had ever heard of. So, I was fully prepared for the equipment, and when I followed Miss Thing downstairs, I just glanced at the stuff.

It was good, I had to admit. But a little ... overdone. Everything was black, unless it was silver (on the buckles and straps). The first room was clearly for her lighter scenes, and for hosting. A refrigerator stood in one corner, and benches lined the walls. I ran a finger across a sturdy wooden chair fitted with thick leather straps. It had been a long time since I had worked with someone who was so equipment- heavy.

The next room had a design suited for a more personal style of play. The centerpiece was a standing bondage cross, clamped to a beam across the ceiling, but a St. Andrew's loomed on one wall, and all sorts of bars, chains, and rings were set into the walls for more interesting arrangements. The only chair in here was clearly for Mistress, comfortable and strapless, with a small square of rubber placed in front of it, for missy's knees, perhaps? One wall held the rows of whips, canes, straps, and paddles, and above them, masks, gags, blindfolds, and trainers. She had enough toys hanging here to stock The Pleasure Chest.

"Your ... guest is here, Mistress," called out Ms. Thing, aiming her voice to the third room. The pause before "guest" made me wonder what she had planned to (had been told to?) say.

"You may go, Jenny. Attend to your chores."

"Yes, Mistress. Thank you Mistress." She bolted, and again I wondered what Surrender had told her to say. I stood where I was, waiting.

"Please disrobe, Kris."

Well, I had no intention to engage in small talk either.

I stripped off my vest first, folding it and placing it in a corner. Then, the boots, jeans, socks, and my uniform shirt. Watch. Wristband. I was left with my collar and a posing strap that went around my waist, covered my sex with a brief triangle, and drew up the back with a thong. It was my normal costume for bottoming in public, although I varied it according to Sir's wishes; sometimes putting the vest back on, sometimes the boots, sometimes wearing a leather jock instead. If I had been very good, the stiff embrace of chaps might cover my legs. I wished I had them in Surrender's playroom.

I stood still again, straightening my back, bracing my legs and locking my hands behind me. I was aware that my stance since I had become a boy was arrogant. I thought of my proud Sir, and a fleeting memory of two nights ago touched me, and I found more strength.

I needed it. Surrender walked into the room, laced into a beautiful corset, boots up to her knee, a silky, flowing skirt dancing around her body as she walked. She was impossibly beautiful, and I ached for her. But behind her, on a leash, wearing shorts and a T-shirt, was Jazz.

I had not expected the boy to be there. And in one second, I realized that I had specified "not public," without saying "no witnesses." It was a tad late for renegotiation. And so it was that the first time I really saw Jazz privately, I was naked, and Jazz was dressed. My first reaction was anger, but I controlled it. As I instinctively drew myself straighter, I drew strength from the memory of the times I had seen Sir bottom in public and how Sir had gained first my interest, then my admiration, and finally my submission. Inwardly, I knew I had a hell of a tough act to follow.

The Triangle

Surrender paused for dramatic effect, and when I didn't drop role to complain about the boy, she continued into the room, and unhooked the leash. Jazz immediately scurried into a corner and knelt, looking into the room, eyes downcast, soft mouth quivering just a little bit. I had just enough time to notice this and wonder about it when Surrender brought me firmly back into focus. She was holding a collar in her hand. Like her many other collars, it was heavy, silver-studded, commercial, and common. Not at all like the elegant, simple band I wore, which bore neither lock nor ring to attach a leash to.

"We are aware to whom you belong, missy"—my lip curled up at the term, but unfortunately I hadn't had the time to go over each distasteful word or phrase she may use with me—"so please remove your collar for this session."

"No, ma'am." I said firmly. "I wear no one else's collar. At *any* time, ma'am."

She clicked her tongue, considering my phrasing, no doubt. We both knew that among those less practiced and less lifestyle-oriented, a refusal to obey was always discourtesy. In this case, I was merely exercising my rights. She turned around, placed the collar on a peg, and sat carefully in her chair, leaning back and laying her arms majestically on the padded rests.

"Very well. Then I shall expect some other form of *obeisance*." She pronounced the word perfectly, sensuously. "Come to me, on your knees."

Carefully, my body dropped. God, I hate crawling! Even for Sir, who so rarely asked it of me. I remembered the words of a professional girl who had told me how she did things she found distasteful.

So, with a cool, almost bored look, I crawled over to the ice bitch, my expression depicting nothing more then a mild interest in what other predictable task she would ask of me. I stopped at a polite distance.

She leaned forward, unexpectedly, and grasped the back of my hair, where it was longest. Savagely, she jerked my head up, causing my mouth to open in a gasp, and planted her crimson lips over mine. I felt her tongue rape my mouth, opening me, tasting me, feeling me moan around her, and as suddenly as she had captured me, she let me free. I fell forward in reflex and caught myself at the last moment, breathing hard.

"I just wanted a taste of you before you used that mouth to good advantage, girl. Let's feel that tongue on my boots, shall we?" And she thrust one elegant booted foot under my face.

"Ma'am"—I caught my breath—"no, ma'am!"

"Are you *defying* me? Are you here to submit, or to play pushy bottom?"

I snapped my head up in anger. *No one* calls *me* a "pushy bottom." "Ma'am, I will kneel to you, I will crawl, but I will not kiss your boots. I am here to submit to you physically, ma'am."

Surprisingly, she smiled, a sight from which I did not take comfort. "Then we shall begin your corporal chastisement, *missy*, and when you are ready for it to stop, you will beg to kiss my boots." This was not a renegotiation. We both knew that I did have a final safe word, one that would stop the action, end the scene, we get dressed, I go home. But she also knew that I had a funny thing about safe words.

I don't like to use them.

Act Four

Surrender made me wait, kneeling and naked, for a good long time while she sent Jazz to fetch equipment.

The Triangle

"The red cat. My driving whip. The screw clamps ... and the box of weights ..."

I watched as Jazz silently gathered these items and more and took them into the next room. After a few minutes of this, I began to tense, as Surrender wanted, so she turned her attention back to me, and stood, making sure her lovely legs brushed against my face as she passed me. She snapped her fingers once and pointed at the bondage cross.

I unfolded myself and approached it, and held my wrists up for the cuffs, one on each arm of the cross. I faced the wood, saw the grain, and then she slipped a leather blindfold over my eyes. As she buckled it with a jerking motion that brought my head back, she said, carefully, in my ear, "I *will* feel that smart mouth of yours on my boots before we end this...." And before I could say anything, I felt the taste of rubber in my mouth, and a ball gag was also buckled on. Blind and silenced, I stood another few minutes, each one longer then the last, as she examined my body, tracing lightly the few marks I still bore from my last caning. Her cool fingers spread my legs, and I felt fumbling hands lock cuffs around my ankles. The boy. She was letting the boy bind me.

I hated her with all my soul.

The first stroke of her short cat was a blessing, because it drew me away from the image of my one day trying to top this creature who had actually helped in my humiliation before this mistress. Instead, I could concentrate, mentally counting as always, on the steady and heavy slap of leather against my back. Surrender didn't seem to be in the mood for foreplay. She used the cat well, and the thumps against my shoulders were steady and aimed very well. I felt each lash and rolled my shoulders to brace for the next. With Sir, I would be moaning for our mutual pleasure. For Surrender, I took it silently, feeling the warmth grow on my shoulders and shoulder blades, and then she switched to my ass.

I fixed my teeth into the gag to swallow, and let her lay into me for a while, standing stock-still. At the first twitch of one leg, she went back to concentrating on my back, and then began to notice the letter appearing on my shoulder.

When she actually stopped hitting me, I fell slightly forward into the restraints, astonished at the sensations. And she was only beginning! I felt her finger trace the initial.

"How interesting ... So this is your famous cutting ... what a waste."

I stopped a protest that would have been a degrading, muffled sound, and stiffened.

"If this had been a brand, it would be much more noticeable. Or a tattoo, perhaps. Was it indicative of your service to Sir that you chose such an impermanent type of mark?"

I pulled back on the cuffs and did let a sound get through the gag, more a growl then an attempt at words. She laughed, and I heard her drop her short cat. In an instant, a heavy leather strap—perhaps a belt—caught me across my ass and threw me against the cross. Six times, my body was thrown forward, each blow with Surrender's full strength behind it, and when she was finished with that, I sagged forward for a moment, my spread legs not affording me much support. Surrender was very strong.

Her body crushed into me from behind, her hand in my hair again, and she said, "Don't you think your mouth has gotten you into enough trouble, missy? I think you remember what to say—or do—when you can't take it anymore!" Shoving my head forward, she snapped her fingers again, and the next thing that made contact with my ass was a paddle. Over and over again, on top of the lash, on top of the strap—god I *hate* paddles—never catching the sweet spot, always in the center, until I could just imagine the color my ass was turning. I finally moaned into the gag, and she stopped.

I heard the jingling sound of chains, and my legs were let free. My arms were next, but before I could reach for the cross for support, a chain was drawn between my two wrist cuffs, and my arms were brought together in front of my body. "Follow!" and a tug, and I stumbled toward the voice, felt her hand on my throat, guiding me, holding my wrists taut, into the next room.

When the mechanics of the move were done, I was standing, barely, on the balls of my feet, my wrists stretched above me. A spreader bar held my ankles apart. From the movement of air around me, I knew I was in the middle of the room. My gag was removed, and a straw was pressed against my lips. I drank the water without giving thanks, and got for my troubles a pair of spring-loaded clips attached to my nipples. When Surrender added weights, I ground my teeth together and made a harsh sound deep in my throat.

"If we can't be polite, missy, we should be silent ..."

Another gag, this time a fake cock.

"And if we believe ourselves to be a *boy,* and we are still *gay,* then the feeling of a male organ in the mouth should be ... *gratifying.*"

And at this point, I realized that I was very, very, wet.

A light nylon whip played all over my body, my legs, thighs, belly, tits, arms, shoulders, back, and ass. She paid a lot of attention to my inner thighs, until I twisted in my bonds, and then went on to my tits.

Each brush of the whip tips made the clamps shudder, and each casual drag of the lashes back across the clip made the weights shake. She switched to a rubber stinger, its slender tresses biting into me like knife edges, until every stroke was a miniature agony. I struggled not to move, calling upon the stubborn strength I was so damn proud of, and sighed heavily around the ersatz prick when she finished. My body throbbed in pain. The dampness spread gradually through my crotch.

When I felt one clothespin on my side, just to the right of my right tit, I didn't worry. With Sir as my guide, I was learning the spiritual strength that comes from a clothespin ritual, where one tries to take as many of the little critters on one's body as possible.

But when the second one followed exactly under it, and then the third and fourth, and fifth, I knew it wasn't just a line of clothespins.

It was a zipper.

A zipper is 12 to 24 clothespins strung on a knotted line, each pin a small distance from the other. With a zipper, the trick is not so much getting them on—but taking them off. They were designed to be pulled off ... jerked off ... at great speed. It was excruciating.

I broke sweat, and felt a bead of it trail down the middle of my back.

Surrender unhurriedly fixed the rest of that string in place and then started one down the inside of my right thigh. Then, down my left thigh. Then on my left side. And then, across the top of my body, across my forward shoulder area, over the tops of my tits. Those pins were the worst, actually, and she moved one when I damn near screamed around her gag.

"We'll just put this one in a better place, missy ... after all, you *will* be wearing these for a while."

The Triangle

And while the front of my body burned with the tiny pain of each individual clothespin, Surrender took up her long, knotted cat and brought up some real color on my back. Unable to keep my balance all the way through the flogging, I fell heavily forward and the weights on my nipple clamps bounced against my body and I screamed, finally, hard and powerfully, the sound muffled but not stopped. Satisfied, she quickly took the nipple clamps off, and got another scream much like the first.

I couldn't believe the multitude of sensations ... the pins, the whip, the agony of the clamps being there, and not being there, the dizziness from being blindfolded, the pain from being stretched ... I panted through my nose, and panicked for a moment, not knowing if I could breathe. But the gag was unbuckled, and I gulped air ... and again, felt the tight wetness between my legs, and I made a motion like a squirm, wishing I could bring my legs together, wishing this were Sir, and I could beg for my daddy's touch, or beg to bring myself off....

... And, like black magic, I felt Surrender's long, cool fingers gently pass the front of my posing strap, and find the proof of my arousal. She chuckled, and worked her fingers under the material, and probed me very, very, gently, and trailed some of my juices up against my stomach.

"What a slut you are, Kris. All this tough talk about being a boy, and look at this ... full of girl-wet, aren't we? All nice and open for Surrender, hmmm?" The fingertips returned, and spread my lips apart, and lightly touched my clit. "This is no cock, missy ... and this is not boy cum, all nasty ... this is nice pussy juice, isn't it, you little butch slut...." The fingers abruptly left my cunt and invaded my mouth, and I tasted myself and moaned. My head dipped forward, against the line of pins across my chest, and I heard the striking hiss of a match.

"Since you're so hot, little girl, I think a touch of wax wouldn't hurt matters any."

The first drop was on my left nipple. I arched my back, bringing my legs under me again, and hissed out my pain. A matching drop on the right nipple got less of a reaction, because I was ready for it. But then Surrender proceeded to drop wax across the head of every clothespin on my body. Covering the business end, where the pin crushed my skin. The sensitive areas, already prepped by the pressure of the pins. I jerked in my chains when she began to do the zippers on my legs, no longer even trying to hide the agony. She planted one boot on the spreader bar to steady me, and continued.

By the time she had finished the line across my chest, real tears had flooded the blindfold, and I was drenched in sweat. I couldn't bear to think about the next step.

And the worst thing about it was that even if I said my safe word now, it wouldn't make much of a difference.

Suddenly the world erupted in pain so sharp that I literally saw stars ... my eyes jerked against the blindfold, and my mouth opened for a scream that was strangled as it began. My entire body shook with the line of red, hot pain that was left when Surrender casually jerked the zipper off my right side. Chips of wax went flying.

"You still think you're so tough, hmmm?" She purred at me, obviously unaware that I was beyond screaming and begging for mercy. I gasped and started to clear my throat, when the zipper on the inside of my right thigh burst into flame ... at least, that was what my mind imagined as she tore it off.

The Triangle

I heard my scream and groan as though it had come from another person, and realized that I was very near my wall, where pain ceased to matter. But I struggled with this, would not allow it, not with *her*. If she managed to get me that far, how would she know how to get me back? I bit my lip, tasted more salt than there should have been, and realized that this was not the first time in this session that I had drawn my own blood. When the zipper on my left side was ripped off, I lost my balance and fell heavily against my wrist cuffs. Only two more ... only two more ...

The one on my left thigh matched the right side in fire, and I screamed again, and felt tears escape the blindfold and begin to track down my cheek. Only one more, only one more ...

And Surrender took her time with that one, pulling them off one ... at ... a ... time. I twisted and groaned, but didn't scream for her again. I heard the lock mechanism of the suspension bar release, and felt her guiding me to the floor, to my knees, and I was grateful for the floor, out of breath, shuddering, shivering, wet and cold and hot and ...

"I think it will be the driving whip next...."

I raised my head a little. "Surrender," I said simply.

She made a cry like a small scream herself. It was my safe word. She was cheated. But no she wasn't, for the next thing I felt was her hand hard against the back of my neck, and I fell face forward, right on top of her boot, my mouth crushed against it. She wiped my lips and teeth across the surface once, and then pulled me back to slam me onto the other. More copper-tasting blood spilled in my mouth as I kept my teeth tightly clenched. She finally let me go with a disgusted hiss.

I fell forward a little more and stretched out, on my belly, ignoring the throbbing from my nipples and sides and thighs and back and ass. Dimly, I heard her snapping commands and saying things, and I tried to concentrate on breathing, on feeling the firm floor beneath my fingers, and I didn't get up until I knew I was alone.

Act Five

"Sixteen."

The finger traced yet another bruise along my hip, and having run out of shivers, my whole body just trembled, silently.

"Seventeen."

I stood in a stance known as the "Saxon Salute" ... my fingers laced at the back of my neck, my legs braced apart, my back stiff. I was getting cold.... Until Sir had noticed the sixth bruise, I had been partially dressed. That was no longer the case.

Sir made a light "tsk" sound as fingers examined, probed gently, and the count went on. Sir had never seen the type of beating I could really take when I had a mind to take it.... Our play was far gentler, and Sir much more skilled in prolonged torment than outright brutality.

"Eighteen. Well, well ... I see you certainly proved how butch you can be, boy."

I blushed under the sarcasm.

"At rest." I brought my arms down. "I hope you understand that I am not at all pleased with the state your body is in."

"Yes, Sir. I'm—I apologize, Sir."

"I do recall ordering you to conclude this without inconveniencing me. Isn't that correct?"

I cringed. "Yes, Sir."

"And the marks on your body should be an inconvenience to me, shouldn't they?"

The Triangle

Should be? I bit my tongue for a moment, knowing Sir's capacity for sadism, and fully knew my capacity to accept discipline for what was really inexcusable behavior. I lowered my head in time to see Sir's boots enter my field of vision. "Yes, Sir," I replied, my voice barely a whisper. Sir grasped my chin and pulled my head up, forcing me to meet two very, very serious eyes.

"If you thought that such marks would be inconvenient, what do you think you should have done, boy?"

"I should have used the safe word ... sooner, Sir. But I——"

Sir cut me off. "No 'buts', boy, just the hard, simple truth. You were too caught up in being tough, and showing off to this little novice you want to impress, so you just forgot your instructions and your responsibility to me, didn't you?"

"I wasn't—I didn't—I just wasn't thinking, Sir."

"This seems to happen to you when you get hard and wet, doesn't it, boy? Answer me."

"Yes, Sir." Oh, yes ... I do get stupid when I'm especially turned on. And despite the gravity of the situation, I could feel my body responding to the cues I was being given. Still stiff and tender, it grew warm in its proximity to my master/tormentor/mentor, and I wanted to bury my face into Sir's shoulder, or hip, or thigh, or boot, and knowing that such comfort would be denied made the waiting all the more delicious. Yes, I was ashamed ... yes, I was contrite ... but behind, above, and through it all, I was hot. Straining, yearning, held back by my own discipline and just about as tense with passion as I could get.

"Well, I should just send you home right now, since your body isn't going to be of much use to me, shouldn't I?"

I looked up for a second in genuine panic. Such a

dismissal would be punishment indeed. And through my embarrassed silence, I found words. "Please, Sir, please, don't send me home! I'm sorry, I really ... let me ... please ..." As suddenly as they appeared, the words vanished, and I let my eyes drop to Sir's belt and then back up again.

"Yes, yes. I suppose you still have some uses. On your knees boy, and put your mouth to work." And, in an instant, there I was, still chilled but only too glad to be presented with an opportunity to prove my worth and redeem myself. I smelled the combined scents of leather, sweat, and Sir's own body and inhaled deeply as I wet my lips, reaching for the flesh I knew so well and adored. The familiar folds of skin were hot and gentle in my mouth, and I groaned into Sir's crotch with my own pleasure, inviting a hand to guide my head, trying not to be too eager, not to be too rushed. I teased and gentled, licked and nibbled, grasped favorite portions gently in my teeth and washed over special areas with the flat of my tongue. Sir seemed impassive above me, but the responses of the flesh showed me how much I was pleasing, and I moaned again, deep in the back of my throat, in thanks and pleasure.

"Oh, you're good, boy ... a damn good little punk ... but we're not letting you off so easy tonight. You know you're going to get your face fucked until you gag, don't you?" A hand closed firmly in my hair and my clit jumped at softly spoken words. Yes ... yes ... I loved servicing Sir and pleasing, but to atone, I wanted to be used, hard and mercilessly, by my gentle Daddy. I wanted to feel the thrusting that I felt when I jerked off, the power controlled and ruthlessly used. I wanted to be utterly available, utterly open, absolutely my Daddy's boy, and I yielded to the guiding hand, relaxing myself.

The Triangle

My Daddy's cock ... so different from mine, in size and texture, but mine fitted a little punk kid. Daddy's cock ... well, was a Daddy's cock. I invited it into my mouth, wetting it, breathing around it, steadied by Sir's hand, and hesitantly, I reached out for Sir's legs.

"Go ahead, boy, grab hold of me. Hold on tight while I fuck your throat...."

A thrust carried the cock right to where Sir called it, and my throat closed once, protectively, around the head. Then, as my body sank lower to allow my neck to arch, I relaxed and took it, relishing the feel of Sir's pubic hairs against my lips and face, the feel of that firm hand in my hair, and the pride in my own ability to take it. As Sir pulled back a little, I breathed around that cock again, my hands grasping Sir's leather-clad legs.

"Good boy ... take it ... that's it, use your mouth...."

And I did. I relaxed as I had taught myself to do, and I took the slow and hard battering of my throat, and with each thrust, I felt a redemption, and a cleansing. I gagged (it's bound to happen), but I recovered and controlled, and allowed my Daddy to use me in whatever way was pleasing. I hugged myself to Sir's legs and drank deeply of scents and tastes, and when I finally choked once too often, I felt my head being drawn back.

"You're a damn good cocksucker, boy."

I wiped at the tears that had formed involuntarily while I was sucking, and said, "Thank you, Sir."

"Now, normally, some mouth-work like that would get you fucked ... but I don't think you'll get that tonight."

Ow. Oh, well, I could have been sent home. I sighed and nodded.

"But I don't think I can let you go without warming your ass a little bit. Not as punishment, but as a reminder."

I was hauled to my feet and bent over, and Sir's hand was swift and harsh against my ass. I cried out and grasped at a leg again to steady myself, my knees stiff from kneeling, my cunt flowing like a damn river.

"You know what I'm reminding you of, boy?"

"My—my responsibilities, Sir...."

"Partly." The hand slapped against my ass several times more, until I was hugging that leg to my cheek, and the sounds I made were more like whimpers than cries of pain.

"This will also remind you that when you forget those responsibilities to the extent that I can't do the things that you love"—each loaded word came with a hard and full slap—"then you go home bruised by an incompetent, and not nearly as pleasured as you like to be with me."

As suddenly as I was thrust down, I was dragged back up, and steadied before Sir, to meet those eyes again, my face flushed with pleasure and shame, my ass barely warmed up, but smarting in some places from Surrender's bruising. Unwanted, there were tears in my eyes again.

"I'm sorry, Sir ... I'm——"

"Shhh. Get dressed."

I went to pick up my clothes, stiff and entirely sexually tense. Even dragging my jeans up over my legs was erotic torment, and the press of Spike against my crotch was maddening. My shirt seemed stiffer then usual over my erect nipples. When I pulled my boots on, the very feel of the leather was agonizing. Had it been so long since I was sent home without a good orgasm? All dressed, I walked back to where Sir was waiting, and I lowered my head.

The Triangle

"Come."

I followed Sir toward the door, and my cunt screamed words at me. My brain was full of suggestions that ranged from throwing myself at Sir's feet and begging, to just pressing myself into Sir's arms and speaking with my body, and my more disciplined mind firmly took control and scolded me for being greedy, and selfish, and for not accepting discipline gracefully and with dignity.

Fuck dignity, answered my cunt.

We were near the door when Sir stopped and turned to me. "Ready to go?"

I swallowed hard and tried to say "Yes, Sir," but my throat refused to let the words out and my incoherent whisper only made things worse. I blushed again and dropped to my knees, wrapping my arms around Sir's hips. I heard myself whispering, "... please, please ..." into the leather, felt my fingers clutching, and my head pounded with a need that outweighed my most stubborn pride.

"It seems my boy has something he wants ... say it!"

"Please, Sir ... please, Daddy ... please forgive me...." Tears came again, and I let them, leaving wet trails along Sir's thigh. I felt Sir's hand at the back of my shirt, pulling me away, and then into my hair, fist clenching and turning my head.

"You're forgiven boy; I think you know that. That's what this is all about, isn't it? You make a mistake ... you are corrected ... you are forgiven. And it's over. It's not a word you want, is it, boy? You want to cum for your Daddy, don't you?"

"Yes! Yes, please, Daddy!"

"And you really thought I'd let you go home like this?" Sir laughed and pulled me up and dragged me over to a table. Standing me up with my back against it, Sir jerked open my fly, buttons parting under one hand, as the other hand pressed me back, onto the table. I moaned as my jeans parted and Sir pulled Spike out of hiding with a harsh tug and thrust the thing against me.

"I wasn't going to send my boy out in all his frustration, not after that nice slave mouth he showed me. Oh no, I accepted that apology ... and now, my boy's gonna cum nice and hard, isn't he?"

I was too busy panting and gasping to answer. Sir's hand firmly guided Spike to that perfect place where my whole cunt could feel the pounding, and the steady thrusting slapped wetly against the open flesh.

"Such a good little boy," Sir's voice continued. "You were going to go on home, your body all ready for pleasure, but being so good, so accepting ... don't you know how good you are?"

I groaned loudly and raised my hips to meet it, and began to breathe in that harsh and low way that signaled my approach to one nice cum. Abruptly, Sir's hand left the cock and fingers slid under the harness to catch and press against my clit. I cried out and arched my back against the table, my legs held apart by Sir's body, my chest held down by Sir's right hand, and I came, shuddering and crying out, and came again, right on the tail of the first, as Sir murmured more encouragements and endearments. As the final spasms subsided, I sat up and buried myself against Sir's chest, whispering rasping thanks.

This time, when we said good night at the door, we had all our good familiarity back, and I hugged my Daddy hard and well before stepping out into the night. Sir's last words to me were, "I'll see you Friday at the Club ... and you can show me this paragon you endured such pain for."

The Triangle

I nodded and left, pleased that Sir wanted to see me work Jazz over. And on my way home, I began to plan what I was sure was going to be my first scene with my own boy.

People are talking about:

The Masquerade Erotic Book Society Newsletter

◆◆◆◆◆◆◆◆◆◆◆◆◆◆◆◆◆◆◆◆◆

FICTION, ESSAYS, REVIEWS, PHOTOGRAPHY, INTERVIEWS, EXPOSÉS, AND MUCH MORE!

◆◆◆◆◆◆◆◆◆◆◆◆◆◆◆◆◆◆◆◆◆

"I received the new issue of the newsletter; it looks better and better."
—*Michael Perkins*

"I must say that yours is a nice little magazine, literate and intelligent."
—*HH, Great Britain*

"Fun articles on writing porn and about the peep shows, great for those of us who will probably never step onto a strip stage or behind the glass of a booth, but love to hear about it, wicked little voyeurs that we all are, hm? Yes indeed...."
—*MT, California*

"Many thanks for your newsletter with essays on various forms of eroticism. Especially enjoyed your new Masquerade collections of books dealing with gay sex."
—*GF, Maine*

"... a professional, insider's look at the world of erotica ..."
—*SCREW*

"I recently received a copy of *The Masquerade Erotic Book Society Newsletter*. I found it to be quite informative and interesting. The intelligent writing and choice of subject matter are refreshing and stimulating. You are to be congratulated for a publication that looks at different forms of eroticism without leering or smirking."
—*DP, Connecticut*

"Thanks for sending the books and the two latest issues of *The Masquerade Erotic Book Society Newsletter*. Provocative reading, I must say."
—*RH, Washington*

"Thanks for the latest copy of *The Masquerade Erotic Book Society Newsletter*. It is a real stunner."
—*CJS, New York*

Free GIFT

WHEN YOU SUBSCRIBE TO:
The Masquerade Erotic Book Society Newsletter

Receive two **MASQUERADE** books of your choice.

Please send me **TWO MASQUERADE BOOKS FREE!**

1. _____

2. _____

☐ I've enclosed my payment of $30.00 for a one-year subscription (six issues) to: **THE MASQUERADE EROTIC BOOK SOCIETY NEWSLETTER.**

Name _____

Address _____

_____ Apt. # _____

City _____ State _____ Zip _____

Tel. ( ) _____

Payment: ☐ Check ☐ Money Order ☐ Visa ☐ MC

Card No. _____

Exp. Date _____

Please allow 4–6 weeks delivery. No C.O.D. orders. Please make all checks payable to Masquerade Books, 801 Second Avenue, N.Y., N.Y., 10017. Payable in U.S. currency only.
Order by phone: 1 800 458-9640 or fax: 212 986-7355.

THE MASQUERADE EROTIC LIBRARY

ROSEBUD BOOKS
$4.95 each

LEATHERWOMEN *edited by Laura Antoniou*
A groundbreaking anthology. These fantasies, from the pens of new or emerging authors, break every rule imposed on women's fantasies, telling stories of the secret extremes so many dream of. The hottest stories from some of today's newest and most outrageous writers make this an unforgettable exploration of the female libido. **3095-4**

BAD HABITS *Lindsay Welsh*
What does one do with a poorly trained slave? Break her of her bad habits, of course! When a respected dominatrix notices the poor behavior displayed by her slave, she decides to open a school: one where submissives will learn the finer points of servitude—and learn them properly. **3068-7**

PASSAGE AND OTHER STORIES *Aarona Griffin*
An S/M romance. Lovely Nina is frightened by her lesbian passions until she finds herself infatuated with a woman she spots at a local café. One night Nina follows her and finds herself enmeshed in an endless maze leading to a mysterious world where women test the edges of sexuality and power. **3057-1**

DISTANT LOVE & OTHER STORIES *A.L. Reine*
In the title story, Leah Michaels and her lover Ranelle have had four years of blissful smoldering passion together. One night, when Ranelle is out of town, Leah records an audio "Valentine," a cassette filled with erotic reminiscences of their life together in vivid, pulsating detail. **3056-3**

PROVINCETOWN SUMMER *Lindsay Welsh*
This completely original collection is devoted exclusively to white-hot desire between women. From the casual encounters of women on the prowl to the enduring erotic bond between old lovers, the women of *Provincetown Summer* will set your senses on fire! **3040-7**

EROTIC *PLAYGIRL* ROMANCES
$4.95 each

WOMEN AT WORK *Charlottte Rose*
Hot, uninhibited stories devoted to the working woman! From a lonesome cowgirl to a supercharged public relations exec, these uncontrollable women know how to let off steam after a tough day on the job. Career pursuits pale beside their devotion to less professional pleasures, as each proves that "moonlighting" is often the best job of all! **3088-1**

LOVE & SURRENDER *Marlene Darcy*
"Madeline saw Harry looking at her legs and she blushed as she remembered what he wanted to do.... She casually pulled the skirt of her dress back to uncover her knees and the lower part of her thighs. What did he want now? Did he want more? She tugged at her skirt again, pulled it back far enough so almost all of her thighs were exposed...." **3082-2**

THE COMPLETE *PLAYGIRL* FANTASIES
The very best—and very hottest—women's fantasies are collected here, fresh from the pages of *Playgirl*. These knockouts from the infamous "Reader's Fantasy Forum" prove, once again, that truth can indeed be hotter, wilder, and *better* than fiction. **3075-X**

DREAM CRUISE *Gwenyth James*
Angelia has it all—a brilliant career and a beautiful face to match. But she longs to kick up her high heels and have some fun, so she takes an island vacation and vows to leave her sexual inhibitions behind. From the moment her plane takes off, she finds herself in one hot and steamy encounter after another, and her horny holiday doesn't end on Monday morning! **30450**

RHINOCEROS BOOKS
$6.95 each

MANEATER *Sophie Galleymore Bird*
Through a bizarre act of creation, a man attains the "perfect" lover—by all appearances a beautiful, sensuous woman but in reality something far darker. Once brought to life she will accept no mate, seeking instead the prey that will sate her supernatural hunger for vengeance. A biting take on the war of the sexes, *Maneater* goes for the jugular of the "perfect woman" myth. **103-9**

THE MARKETPLACE *Sara Adamson*
"Merchandise does not come easily to the Marketplace.... They haunt the clubs and the organizations, their need so real and desperate that they exude sensual tension when they glide through the crowds. Some of them are so ripe that they intimidate the poseurs, the weekend sadists and the furtive dilettantes who are so endemic to that world. And they never stop asking where we may be found...." **3096-2**

VENUS IN FURS *Leopold von Sacher-Masoch*
This classic 19th century novel is the first uncompromising exploration of the dominant/ submissive relationship in literature. The alliance of Severin and Wanda epitomizes Sacher-Masoch's dark obsession with a cruel, controlling goddess and the urges that drive the man held in her thrall. Also included in this volume are the letters exchanged between Sacher-Masoch and Emilie Mataja—an aspiring writer he sought as the avatar of his forbidden desires. **3089-X**

ALICE JOANOU

TOURNIQUET **3067-9**
A brand new collection of stories and effusions from the pen of one our most dazzling young writers. By turns lush and austere, Joanou's intoxicating command of language and image makes *Tourniquet* a sumptuous feast fo rall the senses.

CANNIBAL FLOWER **72-6**
"She is waiting in her darkened bedroom, as she has waited throughout history, to seduce and ultimately destroy the men who are foolish enough to be blinded by her irresistible charms. She is Salome, Lucrezia Borgia, Delilah—endlessly alluring, the fulfillment of your every desire. She will ensnare, entrap, and drive her willing victims to the cutting edge of ecstasy—and then devour them. She is the goddess of sexuality, and *Cannibal Flower* is her haunting siren song."—Michael Perkins

MICHAEL PERKINS

EVIL COMPANIONS 3067-9
A handsome edition of this cult classic that includes a new preface by Samuel R. Delany. Set in New York City during the tumultuous waning years of the 60s, *Evil Companions* has been hailed as "a frightening classic." A young couple explore the nether reaches of the erotic unconscious in a shocking confrontation with the extremes of passion

THE SECRET RECORD: Modern Erotic Literature 3039-3
Perkins, a renowned author and critic of sexually explicit fiction, surveys the field with authority and unique insight. Updated and revised to include the latest trends, tastes, and developments in this much-misunderstood genre.

~

SENSATIONS *Tuppy Owens*
A piece of porn history. Tuppy Owens tells the unexpurgated story of the making of *Sensations*—the first big-budget sex flick. Originally commissioned to appear in book form after the release of the film in 1975, *Sensations* is finally released under Masquerade's stylish Rhino*cer*os imprint. A document from a more reckless, bygone time! **3081-4**

MY DARLING DOMINATRIX *Grant Antrews*
When a man and a woman fall in love it's supposed to be simple, uncomplicated, easy—unless that woman happens to be a dominatrix. This unpretentious love story captures the richness and depth of this very special kind of love. Devoid of sleaze or shame, this is an honest and heartbreaking story of the power and passion that binds human beings together. A must for every serious erotic library. **3055-5**

ILLUSIONS *Daniel Vian*
Two disturbing tales of danger and desire on the eve of WWII. From private homes to lurid cafés to decaying streets, passion is explored, exposed, and placed in stark contrast to the brutal violence of the time. *Illusions* peels the frightened mask from the face of desire, and studies its changing features under the dim lights of a lonely Berlin evening. Unforgettable. **3074-1**

SENSATIONS *Tuppy Owens*
A piece of porn history. Tuppy Owens tells the unexpurgated story of the making of *Sensations*—the first big-budget sex flick. Originally commissioned to appear in book form after the release of the film in 1975, *Sensations* is finally released under Masquerade's stylish Rhino*cer*os imprint. A document from a more reckless, bygone time! **3081-4**

LOVE IN WARTIME *Liesel Kulig*
Madeleine knew that the handsome SS officer was a dangerous man. But she was just a cabaret singer in Nazi-occupied Paris, trying to survive in a perilous time. When Josef fell in love with her, he discovered that a beautiful, intelligent, and amoral woman can sometimes be even more dangerous than the fiercest warrior. A scalding, haunting, and utterly uncompromising look at forbidden passion. **3044-X**

MASQUERADE BOOKS
$4.95 each

GLORIA'S INDISCRETION *Don Winslow*
"He looked up at her. Gloria stood passively, her hands loosely at her sides, her eyes still closed, a dreamy expression on her face ... She sensed his hungry eyes on her, could almost feel his burning gaze on her body, and she was aware of the answering lusty need in her loins...." **3094-6**

HELLFIRE *Charles G. Wood*
A vicious murderer is running amok in New York's sexual underground—and Nick O'Shay, a virile detective with the NYPD, plunges deep into the case. He soon becomes embroiled in an elusive world of fleshly extremes, hunting a madman seeking to purge America with fire and blood sacrifices. But the rules are different here, as O'Shay soon discovers.   **3085-7**

ROSEMARY LANE *J.D. Hall*
The ups, downs, ins and outs of Rosemary Lane, an 18th century maiden named after the street in which she was abandoned as a child. Raised as the ward of Lord and Lady D'Arcy, after coming of age she discovers that her guardians' generosity is truly boundless—as they contribute heartily to her carnal education.   **3078-4**

HELOISE *Sarah Jackson*
A panoply of sensual tales harkening back to the golden age of Victorian erotica. Desire is examined in all its intricacy, as fantasies are explored and urges explode. Innocence meets experience time and again in these passionate stories dedicated to the pleasures of the body. Sweetly torrid tales of erotic awakening!   **3073-3**

MASTER OF TIMBERLAND *Sara H. French*
"Welcome to Timberland Resort," he began. "We are delighted that you have come to serve us. And you may all be assured that we will require service of you in the strictest sense. Our discipline is the most demanding in the world. You will be trained here by the best And now your new Masters will make their choices."   **3059-8**

GARDEN OF DELIGHT *Sydney St. James*
A vivid account of sexual awakening that follows an innocent but insatiably curious young woman's journey from the furtive, forbidden joys of dormitory life to the unabashed carnality of the wild world. Pretty Pauline blossoms with each new experiment in the sensual arts.   **3058-X**

STASI SLUT *Anthony Bobarzynski*
Adina lives in East Germany, far from the sexually liberated, uninhibited debauchery of the West. She meets a group of ruthless and corrupt STASI agents who use her as a pawn in their political chess game as well as for their own gratification until she makes a final bid for total freedom in the revolutionary climax of this *Red*-hot thriller!   **3052-0**

BLUE TANGO *Hilary Manning*
Ripe and tempting Julie is haunted by the sounds of extraordinary passion beyond her bedroom wall. Alone at night she fantasizes about taking part in the amorous dramas of her hosts, Claire and Edward. When she finds a way to watch the nightly debauch, he curiosity turns to full-blown lust, her fantasy becomes flesh,and the uncontrollable Julie goes wild with desire!.   **3037-7**

SEDUCTIONS *Sincerity Jones*
This original collection includes couplings of every variety, including a woman who helps fulfill her man's fantasy of making it with another man, a dangerous liaison in the back of a taxi, an uncommon alliance between a Wall Street type and a funky downtown woman, and a walk on the wild side for a vacationing sexual adventurer. Thoroughly modern women unleashed in these spicey tales.   **83-1**

THE CATALYST *Sara Adamson*
After viewing a controversial, explicitly kinky film full of images of bondage and submission, several audience members find themselves deeply moved by the erotic suggestions they've seen on the screen. Each inspired coupling explorestheir every imagined extreme, as long-denied urges explode with new intensity.   **3015-6**

LUST *Palmiro Vicarion*
A wealthy and powerful man of leisure recounts his rise up the corporate ladder and his corresponding descent into debauchery. Adventure and political intrigue provide a stimulating backdrop for this tale of a classic scoundrel with an uncurbed appetite for sexual power! **82-3**

WAYWARD *Peter Jason*
A mysterious countess hires a tour bus for an unusual vacation. Traveling through Europe's most notorious cities, she picks up friends, lovers, and acquaintances from every walk of life in pursuit of unbridled sensual pleasure. Each guest brings unique sexual tastes and talents to the group, climaxing in countless orgies, outrageous acts, and endless deviation! **3004-0**

ASK ISADORA *Isadora Alman*
Six years of collected columns on sex and relationships. Alman has been called a hip Dr. Ruth and a sexy Dear Abby. Her advice is sharp, funny, and pertinent to anyone experiencing the delights and dilemmas of being a sexual creature in today's perplexing world. **61-0**

LOUISE BELHAVEL

FRAGRANT ABUSES
The sex saga of Clara and Iris continues as the now-experienced girls enjoy themselves with a new circle of worldly friends whose imaginations definitely match their own. Against an exotic array of locations, Clara and Iris sample the unique delights of every country and its culture! **88-2**

DEPRAVED ANGELS
The final installment in the incredible adventures of Clara and Iris. Together with their friends, lovers, and worldly acquaintances, Clara and Iris explore the frontiers of depravity at home and abroad. **92-0**

TITIAN BERESFORD

CINDERELLA
Titian Beresford triumphs again with castle dungeons and tightly corseted ladies-in-waiting, naughty viscounts and impossibly cruel masturbatrixes—nearly every conceivable method of erotic torture is explored and described in lush, vivid detail. **3024-5**

JUDITH BOSTON
Young Edward would have been lucky to get the stodgy old companion he thought his parents had hired for him. Instead, an exqusite woman arrives at his door, and from the top of her tightly-wound bun to the tips of her impossibly high heels, Judith Boston is in complete control. Edward finds his compulsively lewd behavior never goes unpunished by the unflinchingly severe Judith Boston! **87-4**

CHINA BLUE

KUNG FU NUNS
"When I could stand the pleasure no longer, she lifted me out of the chair and sat me down on top of the table. She then lifted her skirt. The sight of her perfect legs clad in white stockings and a petite garter belt further mesmerized me. I lean particularly towards white garter belts." **3031-8**

SECRETS OF THE CITY
China Blue, the infamous Madame of Saigon, a black belt enchantress in the martial arts of love, is out for revenge. Her search brings her to Manhattan, where she intends to call upon her secret sexual arts to kill her enemies at the height of ecstasy. A sex war! **03-3**

HARRIET DAIMLER

DARLING • INNOCENCE
In *Darling*, a virgin is raped by a mugger. Driven by her urge for revenge, she searches New York for him in a furious sexual hunt that leads to rape and murder. In *Innocence*, a young invalid determines to experience sex through her voluptuous nurse. Extraordinary erotic imagination! **3047-4**

THE PLEASURE THIEVES
They are the Pleasure Thieves, whose sexually preoccupied targets are set up by luscious Carol Stoddard. She forms an ultra-hot sexual threesome with them, trying every combination from two-on-ones to daisy chains—but always on the sly, because pleasures are even sweeter when they're stolen! **036-X**

AKBAR DEL PIOMBO

DUKE COSIMO
A kinky, lighthearted romp of non-stop action is played out against the boudoirs, bathrooms and ballrooms of the European nobility, who seem to do nothing all day except each other. **3052-0**

A CRUMBLING FAÇADE
The return of that incorrigible rogue, Henry Pike, who continues his pursuit of sex, fair or otherwise, in the most elegant homes of the most irreproachable and debauched aristocrats. **3043-1**

PAULA
"How bad do you want me?" she asked, her voice husky, breathy. I shrank back, for my desire for her was swelling to unspeakable proportions . "Turn around," she said, and I obeyed, willing to do as she asked. **3036-9**

ROBERT DESMOND

PROFESSIONAL CHARMER
A gigolo lives a parasitical life of luxury by providing his sexual services to the rich and bored. Traveling in the most exclusive circles, this gun-for-hire will gratify the lewdest and most vulgar cravings. Every exploit he performs is described in lurid detail in this story of a prostitute's progress! **3003-2**

THE SWEETEST FRUIT
Connie Lashfield is determined to seduce and destroy pious Father Chadcroft to show her former lover that she no longer requires his sexual services. She corrupts the priest into forsaking all that he holds sacred, destroys his peaceful parish, and slyly manipulates him with her smoldering looks and hypnotic sexual aura. **95-5**

MICHAEL DRAX

SILK AND STEEL
"He stood tall and strong in the shadows of her room, and Akemi lifted up on her pallet to see the man better, hardly able to believe her luck. Akemi knew what he was there for. He let his robe fall to the floor. She could offer no resistance as the shadowy figure knelt before her, gazing down upon her. Why would she resist? This was what she wanted all along...." **3032-6**

OBSESSIONS
Gorgeous Victoria is determined to become a top model by sexually ensnaring the powerful people who control the fashion industry: a voyeur who enjoys photographing Victoria as much as she enjoys teasing him; Paige, who finds herself compelled to watch Victoria's conquests; Pietro and Alex, who take turns and then join in for a sizzling threesome. **3012-1**

LIZBETH DUSSEAU

MEMBER OF THE CLUB
"I wondered what would excite me ... And deep down inside, I had the most submissive thoughts: I imagined myself under the spell of mystery, under the grip of men I hardly knew. If there were a club to join, it could take my deepest dreams and make them real. My only question was how far I'd really go. Did I have the nerve to do the things I imagined? Or was I only kidding myself?" A young woman faces the ultimated temptation. 3079-2

THE APPLICANT
"Adventuresome young woman who enjoys being submissive sought by married couple in early forties. Expect no limits." Hilary answers an ad, hoping to find someone who can meet her special needs. The beautiful Liza turns out to be a flawless mistress, and together with her husband Oliver, she trains Hilary to be the perfect servant. 3038-5

JOCELYN JOYCE

CAROUSEL
A young American woman leaves her husband when she discovers he is having an affair with their maid. She then becomes the sexual plaything of various Parisian voluptuaries. Wild sex, low morals, and ultimate decadence in the flamboyant years before the European collapse. 3051-2

SABINE
One of the most unforgettable seductresses ever. There is no one who can refuse her once she casts her spell. And once ensnared, no lover can do anything less than give up his whole life for her. Great men and empires fall at her feet; but she is haughty, distracted, impervious. It is the eve of WW II, and Sabine must find a new lover equal to her talents and her tastes. A mysterious and erotic force. 3046-6

THREE WOMEN
A knot of sexual dependence ties three women to each other and the men who love them. Dr. Helen Webber finds that her natural authority thrills and excites her high-powered lover Aaron. His daughter, Jan, is involved in an affair with a married man whose wife eases her loneliness by slumming at the local bar with the working guys. A torrid, tempestuous triangle! 3025-3

PRIVATE LIVES
The wealthy French suburb of Dampierre is the setting for this racy soap opera of non-stop action! The illicit affairs and lecherous habits of Dampierre's most illustrious citizens make for a sizzling tale of French erotic life. The wealthy widow who has a craving for a young busboy, who is sleeping with a rich businessman's wife, while her husband is minding his own busines, are just a few of Dampierre's randy residents.

THE WILD HEART
A luxury hotel is the setting for this artful web of sex, desire, and love. A newlywed sees sex as a duty, while her hungry husband tries to awaken her. A Parisian entertains the wealthy guests for the love of money. Each episode provides a new and delicious variation on the old Inn-and-out! 3007-5

DEMON HEAT
An ancient vampire stalks the unsuspecting in the form of a beautiful woman. Unlike the legendary Dracula, this fiend doesn't drink blood; she craves a different kind of potion. When her insatiable appetite has drained every last drop of juice from her victims, she leaves them spent and hungering for more—even if it means being sucked to death! The ultimate in eroti horror. 79-3

HAREM SONG

Young, sensuous Amber flees her cruel uncle and provincial English village in search of a better life, but finds she is no match for the glittering lights and mean streets of London. Soon Amber becomes a classy call girl and is eventually sold into a lusty Sultan's harem—a vocation for which she possesses more than average talent! **73-4**

JADE EAST

Laura, passive and passionate, follows her domineering husband Emilio to Hong Kong. He gives her to Wu Li, a Chinese connoisseur of sexual perversions, who passes her on to Madeleine, a flamboyant lesbian. Madeleine's friends make Laura the centerpiece in Hong Kong's underground orgies—where she watches Emilio recruit another lovely young woman. A journey into sexual slavery! **60-2**

RAWHIDE LUST

Diana Beaumont, the young wife of a U.S. Marshal, is kidnapped as an act of vengeance against her husband. Jack Beaumont sets out on a long journey to get his wife back, but finally catches up with her trail only to learn that she's been sold into white slavery in Mexico. A story of the Old West, when the only law was made by the gun, and a woman's virtue was often worth no more than the price of a few steers! **55-6**

THE JAZZ AGE

This is an erotic novel of life in the Roaring Twenties. A Wall Street attorney becomes suspicious of his mistress when his wife has an interlude with a lesbian lover. *The Jazz Age* is a romp of erotic realism in the heyday of the flapper and the speakeasy. **48-3**

ALIZARIN LAKE

SEX ON DOCTOR'S ORDERS

A chronicle of selfless devotion to mankind! Beth, a nubile young nurse, uses her considerable skills to further medical science by offering incomparable and insatiable assistance in the gathering of important specimens. No man leaves Nurse Beth's station without surrendering exactly what she needs—and none is denied the full attention of this deliciously talented caregiver! A guaranteed cure for all types of fever. **3092-X**

MISS HIGH HEELS

It was a delightful punishment few men dared to dream of. Who could have predicted how far it would go? Forced by his wicked sisters to dress and behave like a proper lady, Dennis Beryl finds he enjoys life as Denise much more! This story of sensuous penalties, wild pleasures, and unexpected switches will surely give life to the fairy tale fantasies that lie behind the most private desires.... **3066-0**

THE INSTRUMENTS OF THE PASSION

All that remains is the diary of a young initiate, detailing the twisted rituals of a mysterious cult institution known only as "Rossiter." Behind sinister walls, a beautiful young woman performs an unending drama of pain and humiliation. What is the impulse that justifies her, night after night, in consenting to this strange ceremony? And to what lengths will her aberrant passion drive her? **3010-5**

FESTIVAL OF VENUS

Brigeen Mooney fled her home in the west of Ireland to avoid being forced into a nunnery. But her refuge in Dublin turned out to be dedicated to a different religion. The women she met there belonged to the Old Religion, devoted to sex and sacrifices. The sex ceremonies of pagan gods! **37-8**

PAUL LITTLE

THE DISCIPLINE OF ODETTE
Odette's family was harsh, but not even whippings and public humiliation could keep her from Jacques, her lover. She was sure marriage to him would rescue her from her family's "corrections." To her horror, she discovers that Jacques, too, has been raised on discipline. An explosive and shocking erotic coupling. **3033-4**

ALL THE WAY
Two excruciating novels from Paul Little in one hot volume! *Going All the Way* features an unhappy man who tries to purge himself of the memory of his lover with a series of quirky and uninhibited women. *Pushover* tells the story of a serial spanker and his celebrated exploits in California. **3023-7**

SLAVES OF CAMEROON
This sordid tale is about the women who were used by German officers for salacious profit. These women were forced to become whores for the German army in this African colony. The most perverse forms of erotic gratification are depicted in this unsavory tale! **3026-1**

THE PRISONER
Judge Black has built a secret room below a women's penitentiary, where he sentences the prisoners to hours of exhibition and torment while his friends watch from their luxurious box seats. Judge Black's House of Corrections is equipped with one purpose in mind: to administer his own brand of rough justice—and sizzling punishments! **3011-3**

THE AUTOBIOGRAPHY OF A FLEA III
That incorrigible voyeur, the Flea, returns for yet another tale of outrageous acts and indecent behavior. This time Flea returns to Provence to spy on the younger generation, now just coming into their own ripe, juicy maturity. With the same wry wit and eye for lurid detail, the Flea's secret observations won't fail to titillate yet again! **94-7**

END OF INNOCENCE
The early days of Women's Emancipation are the setting for this story of some very independent ladies. These girls were willing to go to any lengths to fight for their sexual freedom, and willing to endure any punishment in their desire for total liberation. You've come a long way, baby! **77-7**

CHINESE JUSTICE & OTHER STORIES
Li Woo, the Magistrate of Hanchow, swore to destroy all foreign devils. Then he would subject their women to sexual sports, hanging them upside down from pulleys while his two lesbian torturers applied kisses to their tender, naked flesh. Afterwards, they would perform fellatio on his guests. This is what lay in store for every foreign woman in Hanchow! **57-2**

THE LUSTFUL TURK
In 1814, Emily Bartow's ship was captured by Tunisian pirates. The innocent young bride, just entering the bloom of womanhood, was picked to be held for ransom—but held in the harem of the Dey of Tunis where she was sexually broken in by crazed eunuchs, corrupted by lesbian slave girls and then given to the queen as a sexual toy. Turkish lust unleashed! **28-9**

RED DOG SALOON
Bella Denburg took a vow to avenge her cousin Genevieve, who was kidnapped and raped by Quantrill's Raiders. Bella intended to get herself accepted as a camp follower of Quantrill, find the men responsible, and kill them. Her pursuit led her through whorehouses, rapes, and terrible violence until at last she held each of the guilty ones, unsuspecting, between her legs. Lust and revenge! **68-8**

PASSION IN RIO

For four days and nights during the great Carnival, when all sexual inhibitions are temporarily cast aside, Rio de Janiero goes mad. For lesbian designer Kay Arnold, it begins when the lovely junior designer returns her kiss. For the Porters, the carnival begins when they learn how to satisfy each other. The world's most frenzied sexual fiesta! **54-8**

LUST OF THE COSSACKS

The countess enjoys watching beautiful peasant girls submit to her perverse lesbian manias. She tutors her only male lover in the joys of erotic torture and in return he lures a beautiful ballerina to her estate, where he intends to present her to the countess as a plaything. Painful pleasures abound when innocence encounters corruption! **41-6**

TURKISH DELIGHTS

"With a roar of triumph, Kemil gripped the girl's breasts and forced her back upon the thick rug on the floor.... He went at her like a bull, buffeting her mercilessly, and she groaned ... to her own amazement, with ecstasy!" **40-8**

POOR DARLINGS

Here are the impressions and feelings, the excitement and lust, that young women feel when they submit to desire. Not just with male partners—but with women too. Desperate, gasping, scandalous sex! **33-5**

SLAVE ISLAND

Lord Henry Philbrock, a sadistic genius, has built a hidden paradise where captive females are forced into slavery. They are trained to accommodate the most bizarre sexual cravings of the rich, the famous, the pampered and the perverted. Beyond all civilized boundaries! **3006-7**

CAPTIVE MAIDENS

Three beautiful young women find themselves powerless against the wealthy, debauched landowners of 1824 England. Their masters force them to do their bidding beneath the bite of the whip. For resisting, they are sentenced to imprisonment in a sexual slave colony where they are corrupted into eager participation in every imaginable perversion. Innocent maidens corrupted beyond belief! **3014-8**

MARY LOVE

THE BEST OF MARY LOVE

The very hottest excerpts of this popular writer. Well-known for her outrageous scenes of unbridled sexual indulgence, Mary Love leaves no coupling untried and no extreme unexplored in these selections from *Ecstasy on Fire*, *Vice Park Place*, *Wanda*, and *Naughtier at Night*. There's more than a little satisfying something for everyone in this explosive collection! **3099-0**

ECSTASY ON FIRE

"This was his first time with a woman. He moved his mouth to her instep and kissed it before licking her delicate ankle. Her flesh tasted sweet." An inexperienced young man is taken under wing by the worldy Melissa Staunton—a wildly qualified teacher of the sensual arts. **3086-5**

NAUGHTIER AT NIGHT

"He wanted to seize her. Her buttocks under the tight suede material were absolutely succulent—carved and molded. What on earth had he done to deserve a morsel of a girl like this?" **3030-X**

VICE PARK PLACE

Rich, lonely divorcée Penelope Luckner drinks alone every night, fending off the advances of sexual suitors that she secretly craves. Then she meets Robbie, a much younger man with a virgin's aching appetites, and together they embark on an affair that breaks all their fantasies wide open! **3008-3**

MASTERING MARY SUE

Mary Sue is a rich nymphomaniac whose husband is determined to pervert her, declare her mentally incompetent, and gain control of her fortune. He brings her to a castle in Europe, where, to Mary Sue's delight, they have stumbled on an unimaginably depraved sex cult! **3005-9**

WANDA

Wanda just can't help it. Ever since moving to Greenwich Village, she's been overwhelmed by a desire to be totally, utterly naked! By day, she finds herself inspired by a pornographic novel, at night she parades her quivering, nubile flesh in a nonstop sex show for her neighbors. An electrifying exhibitionist gone wild **3002-4**

ANGELA

Angela's game is "look but don't touch," and she drives everyone mad with desire, dancing for their viewing pleasure but never allowing a single caress. Soon her sensual spell is cast, and she's the only one who can break it! **76-9**

ALEXANDER TROCCHI

HELEN AND DESIRE

Helen Seferis' flight from the oppressive village of her birth became a sexual tour of a harsh world. From brothels in Sydney, to opium dens in Singapore, to shiek's harems in Algiers, Helen chronicles her adventures fully in her diary. Each thrilling encounter is examined in the diary of the sensitive and sensual Helen! **3093-8**

THE CARNAL DAYS OF HELEN SEFERIS

P.I. Anthony Harvest is assigned to save Helen Seferis, a beautiful Australian who has been abducted. Following clues in Helen's explicit diary of sexual adventures, he descends into the depths of white slavery. Through slave markets and harems he pursues Helen, the ultimate sexual prize. **3086-5**

WHITE THIGHS

A dark fantasy of obsession from a modern erotic master. This is the story of young Saul and his sexual fixation on the beautiful, tormented Anna of the white thighs. Their scorching and dangerous passion leads to murder and madness every time they submit. Saul must possess Anna again and again, no matter what or who stands in his way. A disturbing masterpiece! **3009-1**

SCHOOL FOR SIN

When Peggy leaves the harsh morality of her country home behind for the bright lights of Dublin, her sensuous nature leads to her seduction by a stranger. He recruits her into a training school and she embarks on an education in pleasure. No one knows what awaits them at graduation, but each student is sure to be well schooled in sex! **89-0**

YOUNG ADAM

Two British barge operators discover a girl drowned in the river Clyde. Her lover, a plumber, is arrested for her murder. But he is innocent. Joe, the barge assistant, knows that. As the plumber is tried and sentenced to hang, this knowledge lends poignancy to his romances with the women along the river whom he will love then...well, read on . **63-7**

MARCUS VAN HELLER

ADAM & EVE

Adam and Eve long to escape their dull lives by achieving stardom—she in the theater, and he in the art world. Eve soon finds herself acting cozy on the casting couch, while Adam must join a bizarre sex cult to further his artistic career. Everyone has their price in this electrifying tale of ambition and desire! **93-9**

KIDNAP

Nick Harding is called in to investigate a mysterious kidnapping case involving the rich and powerful in London, France, and Geneva. Along the way he has the pleasure of "interrogating" a sensuous exotic dancer named Jeanne and a beautiful English reporter, as he finds himself further enmeshed in the sleazy international crime underworld. A sizzling mystery of sexual intrigue and betrayal! **90-4**

LUSCIDIA WALLACE

FOR SALE BY OWNER

Susie was overwhelmed by the lavishness of the yacht, the glamour of the guests who arrived for the party. But she didn't know the plans Anthony Douglas had for her—training and sale into slavery. How many sweet young women were taught the pleasures of service in this floating prison? How many had suffered the same exquisite punishments? And how many gave as much delight as the newly wicked Susie? **3064-4**

THE ICE MAIDEN

Edward Canton has ruthlessly seized everything he wants in life, with one exception: Rebecca Esterbrook. Frustrated by his inability to seduce her with money, he kidnaps her and whisks her away to his remote island compound, where she learns to shed her inhibitions and accept caresses from both men and women. Fully aroused for the first time in her life, she becomes his writhing, red-hot love slave! **3001-6**

KATY'S AWAKENING

Katy thinks she's been rescued by a kindly couple after a terrible car wreck. Little does she suspect that she's been ensnared by a ring of swingers whose tastes run to domination and wild sex parties. Katy becomes the newest initiate into this private club, and she learns the rules from every player! **74-2**

MASQUERADE READERS

THE COMPLETE EROTIC READER

The very best in erotic writing—from the scandalous to the sublime—come together in a wicked collection sure to stimulate even the most jaded and "sophisticated" palates. All inhibitions are surrrendered, and no desire is left unflaunted in these steamy celebrations of the body erotic. **3063-6**

THE VELVET TONGUE

An orgy of oral gratification! *The Velvet Tongue* celebrates the most mouth-watering, lip-smacking, tongue-twisting action. A feast of fellatio and succulent *soixant-neuf* awaits at this steamy suck-fest. **3029-6**

DOUBLE NOVEL ($6.95)

Two novels of illicit desire, combined into one spellbinding volume! *Lisette Joyaux* tells the story of an innocent young woman seduced by a group of beautiful and experienced lesbians who initiate her into a new world of pleasure. *The Story of Monique* explores an underground society's clandestine rituals and scandalous encounters that beckon to the ripe and willing. **86-6**

A MASQUERADE READER

Masquerade presents a salacious selection of excerpts from its library of erotica. Infamously strict lessons are learned at the hand of *The English Governess* and *Nina Foxton*, where the notorious Nina proves herself a very harsh taskmistress. Scandalous confessions are to be found in *The Diary of an Angel*, and the harrowing story of a woman whose desires drove her to the ultimate sacrifice in *Thongs* completes this collection. **84-X**

INTIMATE PLEASURES

Try a tempting morsel of the forbidden liaisons in *The Prodigal Virgin* and *Eveline*, or the bizarre public displays of carnality in *The Gilded* and *The Story of Monique*, or the insatiable cravings in *The Misfortunes of Mary* and *Darling/Innocence*. **38-6**

LAVENDER ROSE

A classic collection of lesbian erotica: From the writings of Sappho, the queen of the women-lovers of ancient Greece, whose debaucheries on her island have remained infamous for all time, to the turn-of-the-century *Black Book of Lesbianism*; from *Tips to Maidens* to *Crimson Hairs*, a recent lesbian saga. **30-0**

EASTERN EROTICA

DEVA DASI

Dedicated to the cult of the Dasis, the sacred women of India who dedicated their lives to the fulfillment of the senses, this book reveals the secret sexual rites of Shiva. **29-7**

HOUSES OF JOY

A masterpiece of China's splendid erotic literature. This book is based on the *Ching P'ing Mei*, banned many times. Despite its frequent suppression, it has somehow managed to survive—read it and see why! **51-3**

KAMA HOURI

Ann Pemberton, daughter of a British commander in India, runs away with her servant. Forced to live in a harem, she accepts her position and offers herself to any warrior who wishes to mount her. They kindle a fire within her and Ann, sexually ablaze, becomes the legendary white *houri* of the Raj! **39-4**

THE CLASSIC COLLECTION

LADY F.

A wild and uncensored tale of Victorian passions and penalties. Master Kidrodstock suffers deliciously at the hands of the stunningly cruel and sensuous Lady Flayskin—the only woman capable of taming his wayward impulses. Pleasures are paid for dearly in this scorching diary of submission. **102-0**

MAN WITH A MAID

The adventures of Jack and Alice have delighted readers for eight decades! A classic of its genre, *Man with a Maid* tells an outrageous tale of desire, revenge, and submission that is bound to keep yet another generation of readers breathless. **3065-2**

MAN WITH A MAID II

Jack's back! With the assistance of the perverse Alice, he embarks again on a trip through every erotic extreme. Jack leaves no one unsatisfied—least of all, himself, and Alice is always certain to outdo herself in her capacity to corrupt and control. No virtue is safe with these two on the prowl! An incendiary sequel **3071-7**

MAN WITH A MAID: The Conclusion

The final chapter in the saga of lust that has thrilled readers. Jack and Alice seek out new prey to suffer the pleasures of the Snuggery. The adulterous woman who is corrected with enthusiasm and the clumsy maid who receives grueling guidance are just two who benefit from theses lessons! **3013-X**

THE YELLOW ROOM

The "yellow room" holds the secrets of lust, lechery, and the lash. There, bare-bottomed, spread-eagled, and open to the world, demure Alice soon learns to love her lickings. Even more exciting is the second torrid tale of hot heiress Rosa Coote and her adventures in punishment and pleasure with her two sexy, sadistic servants, Jane and Jemima. Feverishly erotic! **96-3**

THE BOUDOIR
Masquerade presents a new edition of the classic Victorian magazine, including several bawdy novellas, ribald stories, and indecent anecdotes to arouse and delight. Six volumes of this original journal of indiscretion are presented here in all their salacious glory. **85-8**

A WEEKEND VISIT
"Dear Jack, Can you come down for a long weekend visit and amuse three lonely females? I am writing at mother's suggestion. Do come!" Fresh from his erotic exploits in *Man with a Maid*, randy Jack is at it again! **59-9**

THE ENGLISH GOVERNESS
When Lord Lovell's son was expelled from his prep school for masturbation, his father hired a very proper governess to tutor theboy—giving her strict instructions not to spare the rod to break him of his bad habits. But governess Harriet Marwood was addicted to domination. The whip was her loving instrument, and with it she taught young Richard to use the rod in ways he had never dreamed. The downward path to perversion! **43-2**

PLEASURES AND FOLLIES
The exploits of a libertine: "Ashamed by excesses provoked by my reading, I compiled a well-seasoned Erotikon and it excited me to such a degree that I ... well, pick up my book and see whether it has a similar effect upon you." A shocking volume chronicling each lurid excess of a man for whom there are no sexual limits! **26-2**

STUDENTS OF PASSION
When she arrives at the prestigious Beauchamp Academy, Francine is young, innocent, and eager to learn. Her teachers and schoolmates enroll her in a course devoted to passion, anatomy, and lust ... and she's determined to graduate with honors. Francine embarks on a course of study sure to leave her breathless! **22-X**

SACRED PASSIONS
Young Augustus comes into the heavenly sanctuary seeking protection from the enemies of his debt-ridden father. Within these walls he learns lessons he coud never have imagined, and soon concludes that the joys of the body far surpass those of the spirit. **21-1**

THE NUNNERY TALES
The Abbess forces her rites of sexual initiation on any maiden who falls into her hands. After exposure to the Mother Superior and her lustful nuns, sweet Emilie, Louise, and the other novices are sexual novices no longer.Each devotes her nubile body to the pursuit of distinctly worldly pleasures. Cloistered concubinage! **20-3**

CLASSIC EROTIC BIOGRAPHIES

THE ROMANCES OF BLANCHE LE MARE
When luscious Blanche loses her husband, it becomes clear she'll need a job. She sets her sights on the stage—and soon encounters a cast of lecherous characters intent on making her path to success as hot and hard as possible! Night after night, Blanche indulges in the pleasures and perversions of her new world, stopping at nothing in her quest to make it *big*. **101-2**

MAUDE RIVERS
A chronicle of the eroic flowering of the lovely Maude. Under the tutelage of her guardian Charles, Maude learns to abandon the restraints of her strict upbringing and embrace the sweet rewards of unbridled sexual indulgence. The lustful Charles leads his lovely charge on an erotic journey of breathtaking variety, and introduces her to a cast of insatiable accomplices. Nothing and no one can stop this lascivious and uncontrollable duo. **3087-3**

KATE PERCIVAL
The memoirs of a blushing maid. Kate, "the Belle of Delaware," divulges the secrets of her scandalous life, from her earliest sexual experiments to the deviations she learns to love. Nothing is secret, and no holes are barred in this titillating tell-all that reveals the hidden lives of turn-of-the-century lads and ladies. 3072-5

THE STORY OF MONIQUE
Lovely, innocent Monique found her aunt's friends strange, curious, inviting. There were seven lesbians who came to Aunt Sonia's parties. And a convent nearby where nuns and monks whipped themselves into a frenzy and then fell upon each other in orgiastic madness. Monique became the mistress of *all* their ceremonies and discovered within herself an endless appetite for sex—the more perverted, the better! 42-4

THE FURTHER ADVENTURES OF MADELEINE
"What mortal pen can describe these driven orgasmic transports?" writes Madeleine as she explores Paris' sexual underground. She discovers that the finest clothes may cover the most twisted personalities of all.—especially of mad monk Rasputin, whose sexual desires match even those of the wicked Madeleine! 04-1

THE MEMOIRS OF MADELEINE
She writes with her cherry-lipped little Fleurette slipping between her legs. She has entertained presidents, kings (and queens). She's Madeleine, the ultimate Parisian courtesan. And now she tells the sexual saga of how she began life in New York City with her sister, cut off without a cent, except for the treasure between her legs. And how she spent it coarsely to become Paris' Queen of the Night. Parisian perversions!

THE AMERICAN COLLECTION

LOVE'S ILLUSION
Elizabeth Renard, local TV news personality, yearned for the body of Dan Harrington, the most desired businessman in the state of California. Then she discovers Harrington's secret weakness: a need to be humiliated and punished. She makes him her slave, and together they commence a journey into depravity that leaves nothing to the imagination—*nothing!* 100-4

THE RELUCTANT CAPTIVE
Sarah is kidnapped by ruthless outlaws who kill her husband and burn their prosperous ranch. Her journey takes her from the bordellos of the Wild West to the bedrooms of Boston, until she is bought at last by a mysterious stranger from her past. 3022-9

LUSTY LESSONS
David Elston had everything—everything except the ability to fulfill the unrelenting demands of his passion. His efforts end in failure until he meets a voluptuous stranger who takes him in hand and leads him to the forbidden land of unceasing pleasure. 31-9

DANCE HALL GIRLS
The dance hall studio in Modesto was ruthless trap for men and women of all ages. They learned to dance under the tutelage of sexual professionals. So grateful were they for the attention, they opened their hearts and their wallets. Scandalous sexual slavery! 44-0

TICKLED PINK
From her spyroom, Emily sees Lady Lovesport, tongue-whip her maid into a frenzy as Mr. Everard enters from behind. Emily is joined in her spying by young Harry, who practices the positions he observes. They become active participants in group sex! An erotic vacation! 58-0

THE GILDED LILY

Lily knows what she wants—pleasure, passion, and new experiences. But more than that, she wants the big break that will launch her career in the movies. She looks for it at Hollywood's most private party, where nothing is forbidden and the only rule is sexual excess. She becomes submerged in a world of secrets and perversions she never imagined. **25-4**

A Very Special Offer
For a Limited Time Only!

Masquerade Books is proud to present a volume of unparalleled artistry in the field of erotica. *The Journal of Erotica, Volume One* is unquestionably the most stunning collection of erotic art, writing, and photography to be published in the last 30 years.

This sturdy, handsomely bound and embossed volume includes incisive, entertaining fiction and over 80 pages of provocative photography (including 43 full-color plates). From some of the earliest sexual images ever exposed on film (circa 1855), to the seductive, streetwise, and very contemporary work of Katarina Jebb, *The Journal of Erotica* is a feast for the eyes.

The Journal of Erotica will surely be regarded as the most unique and collectible publication since *Eros* burst on the scene in the 60s. No erotic library is complete without it; no afficianado will want to miss it.

The Journal of Erotica, Volume One lists at $25.00—but is available to you for $19.95 a copy (plus $2.50 shipping & handling). Only a limited number are available. Call toll-free: 1 800 458-9640, or fax your order: 212 986-7355.

THE MASQUERADE LIBRARY

Title	Code	Price
SECRETS OF THE CITY	03-3	$4.95
THE FURTHER ADVENTURES OF MADELEINE	04-1	$4.95
THE GILDED LILY	25-4	$4.95
PLEASURES AND FOLLIES	26-2	$4.95
STUDENTS OF PASSION	22-X	$4.95
THE NUNNERY TALES	20-3	$4.95
DEVA-DASI	29-7	$4.95
THE STORY OF MONIQUE	42-4	$4.95
THE ENGLISH GOVERNESS	43-2	$4.95
POOR DARLINGS	33-5	$4.95
LAVENDER ROSE	30-0	$4.95
KAMA HOURI	39-4	$4.95
THONGS	46-7	$4.95
THE PLEASURE THIEVES	36-X	$4.95
SACRED PASSIONS	21-1	$4.95
LUST OF THE COSSACKS	41-6	$4.95
THE JAZZ AGE	48-3	$4.95
MY LIFE AND LOVES (THE 'LOST' VOLUME)	52-1	$4.95
PASSION IN RIO	54-8	$4.95
RAWHIDE LUST	55-6	$4.95
LUSTY LESSONS	31-9	$4.95
FESTIVAL OF VENUS	37-8	$4.95
INTIMATE PLEASURES	38-6	$4.95
TURKISH DELIGHTS	40-8	$4.95
JADE EAST	60-2	$4.95
A WEEKEND VISIT	59-9	$4.95
RED DOG SALOON	68-8	$4.95
HAREM SONG	73-4	$4.95
KATY'S AWAKENING	74-2	$4.95
CELESTE	75-0	$4.95
ANGELA	76-9	$4.95
END OF INNOCENCE	77-7	$4.95
DEMON HEAT	79-3	$4.95
TUTORED IN LUST	78-5	$4.95
DOUBLE NOVEL	86-6	$6.95
LUST	82-3	$4.95
A MASQUERADE READER	84-X	$4.95
THE BOUDOIR	85-8	$4.95
SEDUCTIONS	83-1	$4.95
FRAGRANT ABUSES	88-2	$4.95
SCHOOL FOR SIN	89-0	$4.95
CANNIBAL FLOWER	72-6	$4.95
KIDNAP	90-4	$4.95
DEPRAVED ANGELS	92-0	$4.95
ADAM & EVE	93-9	$4.95
THE YELLOW ROOM	96-3	$4.95
AUTOBIOGRAPHY OF A FLEA III	94-7	$4.95
THE SWEETEST FRUIT	95-5	$4.95
THE ICE MAIDEN	3001-6	$4.95
WANDA	3002-4	$4.95
PROFESSIONAL CHARMER	3003-2	$4.95
WAYWARD	3004-0	$4.95
MASTERING MARY SUE	3005-9	$4.95
SLAVE ISLAND	3006-7	$4.95
WILD HEART	3007-5	$4.95
VICE PARK PLACE	3008-3	$4.95
WHITE THIGHS	3009-1	$4.95
THE INSTRUMENTS OF THE PASSION	3010-5	$4.95
THE PRISONER	3011-3	$4.95

Title	Code	Price
OBSESSIONS	3012-1	$4.95
MAN WITH A MAID: The Conclusion	3013-X	$4.95
CAPTIVE MAIDENS	3014-8	$4.95
THE CATALYST	3015-6	$4.95
SINS OF THE CITIES OF THE PLAIN	3016-4	$4.95
A SECRET LIFE	3017-2	$4.95
YOUTHFUL DAYS	3018-0	$4.95
IMRE	3019-9	$4.95
TELENY	3020-2	$4.95
THE SCARLET PANSY	3021-0	$4.95
THE RELUCTANT CAPTIVE	3022-9	$4.95
ALL THE WAY	3023-7	$4.95
CINDERELLA	3024-5	$4.95
THREE WOMEN	3025-3	$4.95
SLAVES OF CAMEROON	3026-1	$4.95
MEN AT WORK	3027-X	$4.95
MUSCLE BOUND	3028-8	$4.95
THE VELVET TONGUE	3029-6	$4.95
NAUGHTIER AT NIGHT	3030-X	$4.95
KUNG FU NUNS	3031-8	$4.95
SILK AND STEEL	3032-6	$4.95
THE DISCIPLINE OF ODETTE	3033-4	$4.95
THE SEXPERT	3034-2	$4.95
MIKE AND ME	3035-0	$4.95
PAULA	3036-9	$4.95
BLUE TANGO	3037-7	$4.95
THE APPLICANT	3038-5	$4.95
THE SECRET RECORD	3039-3	$4.95
PROVINCETOWN SUMMER	3040-7	$4.95
MR. BENSON	3041-5	$4.95
SLOW BURN	3042-3	$4.95
CRUMBLING FAÇADE	3043-1	$4.95
LOVE IN WARTIME	3044-X	$4.95
DREAM CRUISE	3045-8	$4.95
SABINE	3046-6	$4.95
DARLING • INNOCENCE	3047-4	$4.95
THE HEIR • THE KING	3048-2	$4.95
BADBOY FANTASIES	3049-0	$4.95
STASI SLUT	3050-4	$4.95
CAROUSEL	3051-2	$4.95
DUKE COSIMO	3052-0	$4.95
TALES FROM THE DARK LORD	3053-9	$4.95
SLAVES OF THE EMPIRE	3054-7	$4.95
MY DARLING DOMINATRIX	3055-5	$4.95
DISTANT LOVE	3056-3	$4.95
PASSAGE & OTHER STORIES	3057-1	$4.95
GARDEN OF DELIGHT	3058-X	$4.95
MASTER OF TIMBERLAND	3059-8	$4.95
TOURNIQUET	3060-1	$4.95
THE SWITCH	3061-X	$4.95
SWEET DREAMS	3062-8	$4.95
THE COMPLETE EROTIC READER	3063-6	$4.95
FOR SALE BY OWNER	3064-4	$4.95
MAN WITH A MAID	3065-2	$4.95
MISS HIGH HEELS	3066-0	$4.95
EVIL COMPANIONS	3067-9	$4.95
BAD HABITS	3068-7	$4.95
GOLDEN YEARS	3069-5	$4.95
REUNION IN FLORENCE	3070-9	$4.95
MAN WITH A MAID II	3071-7	$4.95
KATE PERCIVAL	3072-5	$4.95
HELOISE	3073-3	$4.95

ILLUSIONS	3074-1	$4.95
THE COMPLETE *PLAYGIRL* FANTASIES	3075-X	$4.95
DEADLY LIES	3076-8	$4.95
B.M.O.C.	3077-6	$4.95
ROSEMARY LANE	3078-4	$4.95
MEMBER OF THE CLUB	3079-2	$4.95
ECSTASY ON FIRE	3080-6	$4.95
SENSATIONS	3081-4	$4.95
LOVE AND SURRENDER	3082-2	$4.95
THE ARENA	3083-0	$4.95
BAYOU BOY	3084-9	$4.95
HELLFIRE	3085-7	$4.95
THE CARNAL DAYS OF HELEN SEFERIS	3086-5	$4.95
MAUDE CAMERON	3087-3	$4.95
WOMEN AT WORK	3088-1	$4.95
VENUS IN FURS	3089-X	$4.95
SORRY I ASKED	3090-3	$4.95
LEWD CONDUCT	3091-1	$4.95
GLORIA'S INDISCRETION	3094-6	$6.95
HELEN AND DESIRE	3093-8	$4.95
SEX ON DOCTORS ORDERS	3092-X	$4.95
THE MARKET PLACE	3096-2	$4.95
THE SEXUAL ADVENTURES OF SHERLOCK HOLMES	3097-0	$4.95
STOLEN MOMENTS	3098-9	$4.95
LEATHER WOMEN	3095-4	$4.95

COMING SOON FROM
MASQUERADE BOOKS

The Wet Forever
David Aaron Clark

Sensuous/Magic
Pat Califia

The Marco Vassi Collection

ORDERING IS EASY!

MC/VISA orders can be placed by calling our toll-free number

PHONE 800-458-9640 / FAX 212 986-7355

or mail the coupon below to:

Masquerade Books 801 Second Avenue New York, New York. 10017

BUY ANY FOUR BOOKS AND CHOOSE ONE ADDITIONAL BOOK AS YOUR FREE GIFT.

QTY.	TITLE	LW 095-4	NO.	PRICE
		SUBTOTAL		
		POSTAGE & HANDLING		
		TOTAL		

Add $1.00 Postage and Handling for tthe first book and 50¢ for each additional book. Outside the U.S. add $2.00 for the first book, $1.00 for each additional book. New York state residents add 8-1/4% sales tax.

NAME _____

ADDRESS _____ APT. # _____

CITY _____ STATE _____ ZIP _____

TEL. ( ) _____

PAYMENT: ❑ CHECK   ❑ MONEY ORDER   ❑ VISA   ❑ MC

CARD NO. _____ EXP. DATE _____

PLEASE ALLOW 4–6 WEEKS DELIVERY. NO C.O.D. ORDERS. PLEASE MAKE ALL CHECKS PAYABLE TO MASQUERADE BOOKS. PAYABLE IN U.S. CURRENCY ONLY